The engine revved and Jonas stepped away to let the car go...

"But to his surprise, it didn't move. Instead, he saw a finger cut a line through the window fog. A message began to form. Jonas breathed the words as he read them:

PHANTOM
STRIKES
TONIGHT

When the message was finished, the car roared off around the bend."

written and illustrated by Wolfgang Parker

BOOK ONE

CRIME CATS

THE DUSENBURY CURSE

Neil Higgins   CatBob

CRIME CATS

THE DUSENBURY CURSE

WRITTEN & ILLUSTRATED BY **WOLFGANG PARKER**

EDITED BY **BEN SOSTROM**

I would like to express my gratitude to the following friends.
Their contributions and support have made this book possible.

Kitty Maer, Ben Sostrom, Doug Clay, Ross Hughes, Alycia Yates,
Gail Harbert and Cat Welfare of Ohio Association, Trey Hammanthorn
and the Clintonville Co-op crew, Melissa Goodrich, Olivera Bratich, Amy D,
Sally Oddi, Gib and the Laughing Orge crew, the CresFest crew, Vinnie "Mad
Chain" Maneri, Regan and Jonas Tonti, everyone who bought *Missing* and the
cats of Clintonville and their wonderful families.

CRIME CATS: THE DUSENBURY CURSE

RL 4. 008—012

Third Printing, 2015

ISBN 978-0692318065

15 14 13 12 11 10 / 10 9 8 7 6 5 4 3

PRINTED IN THE UNITED STATES OF AMERICA

To Kitty and Sascha:

For your constant entertainment, inspiration, and encouragement.

~ W.P.

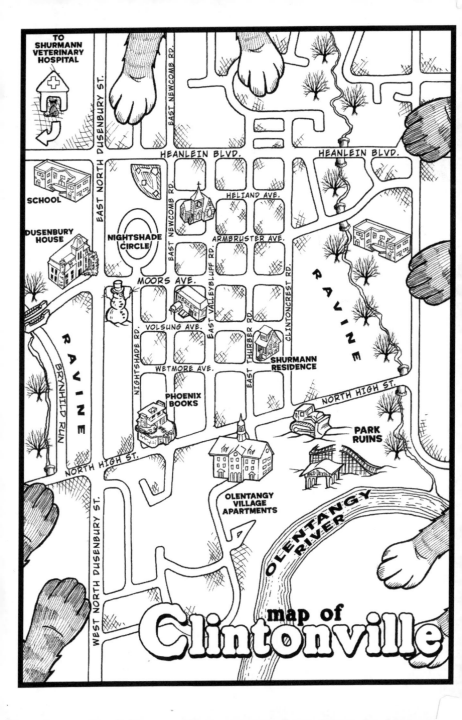

map of Clintonville

PROLOGUE

Ondine was sure she had seen something skitter across the snow and dive into a thicket of tall brown grass. The shaggy black and white cat crept closer, watching the tall blades for the slightest quiver that might reveal her prey. A moment later, she spied a small furry face. It peeked out from the thicket and sniffed at the frigid air. Ondine's claws dug into the snow until her back feet were firmly planted against the hard ground. She lifted her butt and wiggled it, preparing to pounce. But before she leaped, a distant cry broke her concentration.

"Ondine! Ondine!" Breathless meows came echoing through the snowdrifts.

The shaggy cat stood up to find her friend Lucy clomping through the snow toward her. "Be quiet, Lucy, you're scaring the food away!" she called. But her rotund friend didn't stop meowing. Ondine could see she was in a panic. "All right, take it easy, Luce." Ondine said. "What's the matter?"

"Machines... " Lucy gasped between coughing fits. "...At the gates."

A nearby group of cats froze as they caught her words. They muttered to each other and ran back toward the trees.

"The machines are back?" Ondine asked. "You're sure?"

Lucy nodded. "Come see for yourself!" The gray feline barreled down a winding path that ended at a set of rusty gates that hung crooked from its hinges. Beyond the chain links, the pair could see an enormous yellow machine churning through the snow toward them. The metal beast's claws ripped chunks from the ground and black smoke billowed from its ears every time it roared. The felines crouched low and growled.

"We need to get back to the house!" Ondine cried.

The pair turned and bolted back up the winding trail toward the trees. They loped through the snow to a large stone house that sat huddled at the edge of a wood. An empty window frame next to the front door provided a snug entrance into the dreary domain. Inside, the felines climbed a staircase and disappeared behind an open door, where they paused to sniff at the food scraps that littered the floor.

"Do you think she already knows?" Lucy whispered.

"Knows what?" a voice boomed from the darkness.

Lucy shrieked as a pair of shining blue eyes blinked open only inches from her snout. "We were just going to tell you—the, the—" she stammered.

"The machines have returned." Ondine said.

The eyes hovered unblinking in the gloom.

"You can stop them, can't you?" Lucy asked timidly.

"Of course," the voice answered coldly. "To stop the machines we need only stop the one who controls the machines."

"But who controls the machines?" Ondine said.

"Dusenbury," the voice replied.

1
PEE-PEE CAT

"Curses!" Mr. Shurmann yelled.

Jonas and his father had spotted the tendrils of smoke creeping from the oven at the same time. Jonas's dad stuffed his hand into an oven mitt and yanked the door open. The kitchen was instantly filled with a black cloud that set the smoke detector into a fit. Mr. Shurmann choked out apologies to Jonas as he tried to fan the smog toward an opened window with a cutting board. After a few minutes, the haze began to thin and the alarm fell silent once again.

"Sorry about that," Mr. Shurmann said. "I thought I set the timer. At least we know the smoke detector works, right?" The hexagonal lenses of his eyeglasses were fogged. He wiped them on his shirt and frowned at the smoldering remains of what was supposed to be a batch of chocolate chip cookies.

"Well, I *was* saving the other package of dough for later, but if your mother makes it through all this snow and finds there are no cookies waiting for her, your father will be *very* sorry."

Freshly baked cookies during a snowstorm were a Shurmann family tradition that began when Jonas's mom was a kid. Even though Mrs. Shurmann didn't normally care for sweets, the sight of snow always triggered a sudden craving for her mom's freshly baked chocolate chip cookies. Mr. Shurmann glanced down at his cell phone and saw that it was about the time his wife normally left Shurmann Veterinary Hospital for home. Jonas opened the refrigerator and tossed the other package of dough to his dad.

"Thanks, Bud," Mr. Shurmann said as he tore open the package. "You'd better go on upstairs so I can get this mess cleaned up before your mom gets home."

"Be sure to get rid of the evidence," Jonas said.

"Oh, yeah." His dad snatched the sheet from the counter and opened the back door. With a quick flick, the smoking hunks of ash went sailing into a snowdrift. He quickly closed the door and straightened up. "Well, with any luck, it'll be spring before she gets wise to this one," he said with a sly smile.

"Smooth, Dad." Jonas giggled.

Mr. Shurmann replied with a wink and a nod.

"Go on," he said, "I think things are sufficiently out of control down here."

"Call me when they aren't burnt!" Jonas yelled as he scrambled up the stairs to his room. He walked in to discover his ceiling light had burned out. When the wall switch failed to ignite the bulb Jonas just shrugged and shuffled over to his bedroom window. The darkened room allowed him a clear view of East Thurber Road, or what used to be East Thurber Road. Five inches of snow had fallen in the last three hours and his street, along with the rest of Clintonville, was almost unrecognizable—even to Jonas, who had lived there all eight years of his life.

He was giddy with excitement. Jonas always got excited when there was a big snowstorm because that meant there was a chance that school would be canceled the next day. Instead of sitting in the classroom listening to Miss Keys, he would be free to spend the day sledding, building snowmen and forts, and getting in snowball fights with the other kids. But even if school wasn't canceled, Jonas found the Snow World was way more fun than the normal one.

When his neighborhood was buried under a lot of snow, Jonas found it easy to imagine he was actually in a different place—or even in a different world. He often pretended to be an astronaut who had crash-landed alone on an alien planet. Although he had

3

never told anyone about it, this was Jonas's favorite wintertime game. In fact, he had so much fun playing and exploring that the first couple of days after the storm felt like a vacation. Unfortunately, his two best friends didn't share his love of snowstorms.

CatBob and Neil Higgins preferred spending the cold winter months sleeping on heating vents and watching the snow from the comfort of their homes, as most cats do. But CatBob and Neil weren't just regular cats; they were real-life detectives. And along with Jonas, the trio had become local heroes the previous autumn when they managed to find a dozen missing cats and return them to their families. Neighbors on the *Clintonville Social Network* had dubbed Jonas the Chicken-Boy of Clintonville—on account of the chicken costume he wore—and nicknamed his partners the Crime Cats. Since then, the Chicken-Boy and the Crime Cats had continued to find and return lost animals to their families.

When animal-friends went missing, the first thing their families did was post about it on the Network's *Lost and Found Furry Friends* group. Jonas would then copy their post to the official Crime Cats profile. This enabled their followers to help the detectives by checking around their yards and garages. Afterward, Jonas would slip into his chicken costume and meet up with his partners.

Jonas's costume gave him the power to communicate with cats. He didn't know how, just that it did. And it was through this magic power that he met his partners.

So far, the trio had helped more than two dozen cats find their way back home, and they were always on the lookout to help anyone in need.

But presently, Jonas saw no calls for help on his News Feed. It was clogged with posts from adults complaining about the snow. Apparently when you grow up, you're not allowed to play in the snow anymore. Jonas sniffed. There was no way *he* was ever going to stop playing in snow, no matter how old he got.

A chime sounded. A new notification popped up on the screen. Jonas's good friend, Orville Dusenbury, was trying to contact him with an Instant Message. Orville was an adult who lived alone in a run-down mansion that all the neighborhood kids thought was haunted. The trio had met him during their investigation into the missing cats. In fact, the trio had become such good friends with him that CatBob and Neil were presently staying at the mansion while their families were away.

Jonas clicked the "accept" button and his computer screen was suddenly filled with the image of a big cat butt. Jonas giggled. He could tell the gray butt belonged to his friend and partner, Neil Higgins. A hand pushed the butt out of the frame and Orville's bearded face appeared.

"He's on, Neil," Orville said. "Turn around. He doesn't want to see your big fuzzy trunk!"

Despite the fact that most of Orville's face was hidden under a bushy Afro and a long beard, Jonas could still tell his friend was in a bad mood. Orville's eyebrows were contorted in the shape of an *M* on his wrinkled forehead.

Neil turned to face the computer. The round gray cat meowed his greetings and touched his nose to the screen.

"Hey, guys!" Jonas exclaimed. "How are things at Castle Dusenbury? Are you keeping warm? Where's CatBob?"

"I don't know *where* CatBob is right now," Orville grumbled. "I just got home a little while ago and I've been too busy cleaning up pee-pee to notice."

"Pee-pee?" Jonas exclaimed. "Whose pee-pee?"

"CatBob's!" Orville said. "If I had known I was hosting a Pee-Pee Cat sleepover, I would have covered the house in plastic sheets."

"He's spraying in the house?" Jonas asked. "That's not normal. How many times has he peed so far?"

"I don't know," Orville sighed, "a few. But that's

a few too many! Castle Dusenbury doesn't need any more problems than it already has. You might have to come and get him."

Jonas fell back in his chair. "I'm sorry, Orville. He's never done that here. I wouldn't let him over there if he did." He felt terrible that CatBob had been peeing in his host's house. But as much as he didn't like to see Orville upset, he was more concerned that CatBob's spraying could be a sign of a serious health issue. Jonas knew from working for his mom at her veterinary hospital that cats oftentimes pee outside of their litter box to signal to their family that something is wrong. And sometimes, the illnesses that cause them to do it are fatal.

Suddenly, there was a crash. Orville leaped from his chair and yelled. "I don't know what you're up to," he bellowed, "but there had better not be more pee-pee!" He stomped off-screen toward the noise.

"What's going on, Neil?" Jonas asked quietly.

The one-eyed feline shook his head. "I have no idea. Everything was fine yesterday, but this afternoon I found CatBob staring out of a window that overlooks the yard and he hasn't left the spot since. Well, until Orville discovered the puddle. I looked out the window to see for myself what he'd been watching, but I didn't see anything but snow."

"Is it just him peeing or are you both doing it?"

Jonas asked.

"Not I," Neil scoffed. "Orville's a wonderful host. The litter here is made from *wheat*. It doesn't stink like the normal stuff. It's so soft—like doing my Secret Butt Stuff in a freshly-dug garden!" The gray cat sighed and added, "I'm afraid it's all Bob. I don't know what's gotten into him. He doesn't look or smell sick to me, so I don't think it's a physical ailment."

Jonas knew that Neil was smart—smarter than most humans—and hearing Neil say he doubted Cat-Bob was sick eased his worry. But his anxiety was soon replaced with anger when he thought about how upset CatBob had made Orville.

"Well, he's being a big jerk!" Jonas spat. "Orville's been nothing but nice to us and he doesn't deserve to have Castle Dusenbury peed all over." Jonas leaned toward the screen and added, "Especially since having you two stay while your families are out of town was supposed to cheer him up. But CatBob wizzing in the house makes us all look like ungrateful jerks. I guess I'm gonna to have to—"

Jonas stopped when he heard another chime. He looked down and saw another Message notification. "Now what?!" he muttered. "Is Orville going to say CatBob took another wizz on something?" He clicked on the link and another window opened. But instead of a video image, there was just a white screen with a short message spelled out. The sender's name was PHOENIX. The message read:

BEWARE THE WHITE PHANTOM

"By the way," Neil continued, "Orville has a subscription to science magazines and they are fascinating—" but Jonas cut him off.

"Hang on, Neil." Jonas read the message again. He didn't know anyone that called himself PHOENIX. Jonas typed a reply:

WHO IS THIS?

CATBOB, came the reply.

YOU'RE NOT CATBOB, Jonas typed.

Three quick replies followed.

WHITE PHANTOM

HAS

CATBOB

2
THE HOODED FIGURE

Jonas's heart sank as he reread the message.

Another chime rang out. A notification stated that PHOENIX had left the conversation.

Jonas looked up at Neil. "Where is CatBob?!" he asked.

"Probably at the window again." Neil said. "Orville left to find him, but—"

"You need to find him—now!" Jonas said.

Just then Orville reappeared. He collapsed back into his chair and frowned. "I don't know what that crazy cat is up to now," he sighed. "I can't find him anywhere. At least I didn't find more pee-pee."

"You have to look again!" Jonas shouted as he leaped from his seat. "I think CatBob's in trouble. I'm coming over now."

"Trouble?" Orville leaned into the screen.

"What's going on, Drumsticks?"

"I'll tell you when I get there. Just go find him—right now!" Jonas snatched his chicken feet off the bed and jammed them on. He was rushing to the door when something caught his attention and made him pause. He walked over to the window and peered down into the street again.

Jonas spied an odd glow amid the falling sheets of snowflakes. He pressed his face to the cold glass and squinted. There was a dark figure standing near the street that hadn't been there before. It clutched a phone in its hands. It was the eerie glow from the phone's screen that Jonas had noticed. But despite the ghostly light, a large hood hid the person's face from view. The Hooded Figure looked up at Jonas and then quickly hurried away.

Jonas scrambled downstairs and set to work shoving his arms into his coat. He tugged his hood up, shoved his hands into his gloves, and called to his dad that he would be right back. Before Mr. Shurmann could reply, Jonas had plunged through the door and into the storm.

Jonas found he could run in the snow more easily in his chicken feet than he could in his snow boots. The costume feet acted like snowshoes, distributing his weight more evenly across the snow's surface, which prevented his feet from sinking. He

ran through the swirling flakes to the sidewalk, where he discovered fresh footprints leading around the corner. He followed the prints until they disappeared where a fresh set of tire tracks began. The tracks cut down the street, into the darkness.

"Aww, man!" Jonas cried. "No fair!" He heard a squeak of rusted metal. A set of car taillights blinked on a block away. He broke into a run, huffing the frigid air as he stomped toward the vanishing lights.

"Hey!" he yelled, "Wait up!" Jonas managed to follow the brake lights down Volsung Avenue and up East Newcomb Road before he was forced to stop to catch his breath.

He was burning up under his coat. Rivulets of melting snow trickled into Jonas's eyes. He swiped at his face with his gloves as he stumbled onto Moors Avenue. There, he caught sight of the taillights just as they disappeared into an alley that ran behind the south side of East North Dusenbury Street.

Jonas's legs began to wobble as he staggered to a stop midway down the alley. He bent over to catch his breath. As he did, he spied something lying in the snow at his feet. It was a body. A small body. Jonas's gloves uncovered a peach-colored tail that came to a crooked end. Jonas gasped. It was his friend, CatBob!

Jonas called to the unconscious feline, but his

friend remained still. There was blood on his fur, but Jonas could see he was still breathing. Jonas scooped up his partner and tucked him inside his coat, then stumbled to his feet, and forced his tired legs on toward Castle Dusenbury.

Ahead of him, a maroon station wagon slowed to a stop at the mouth of the alley. The Hooded Figure sat behind the wheel. It turned to face Jonas just before the car lurched away with a throaty roar. Jonas stumbled forward, trying to get a good look at the driver, but his shaking legs refused to carry him quickly enough. He did, however, manage to catch sight of the vehicle's license plate.

It read PHOENIX.

3
THE CHASE

Jonas gritted his teeth. Every muscle in his body burned. He was exhausted from chasing the Hooded Figure's station wagon, but there was no time to rest. He gently cradled CatBob in his coat as he staggered on toward Castle Dusenbury. By the time he climbed onto the doorstep, his legs were trembling. He could barely manage to muster enough strength to kick the door. But soon after he did, Orville and Neil ushered him out of the cold.

Once inside, Jonas handed CatBob to Orville, and then collapsed into a crumpled heap on the floor. Orville and Neil took CatBob into the living room and laid the unconscious feline on a blanket in front of a cozy fire. Neil set to work fussing over his friend while Orville returned to check on Jonas.

"You okay, Drumsticks?" Orville asked.

Jonas lolled his tongue out of the side of his mouth. "It hurts," he moaned.

"What hurts?"

Jonas swept his hand from his head to his feet. "This," he whined. "*All* of this."

"So, is this the end of the Chicken-Boy?" Orville asked. "Are we finally gonna need that bucket?"

Jonas waved him off. "Never! I'm made of steel," he gasped. "But you've gotta call my mom. She needs to get over here right away. CatBob's really hurt."

"On it!" Orville said as he reached into his pants pockets. He paused. "What the—?" He patted his shirt pocket and sweater pockets, then sighed. "Where's my—Ugh!" He turned on his heels and ran down the hall.

Jonas heaved himself up off the floor and yanked his hood back. A shiver racked his body. The clothes under his coat were sweat-drenched and cold. He peeled out of what he could and tossed the discarded articles onto a floor vent. While wrestling out of his gear, Jonas noticed a pile of unopened letters on a small table by the door. The letters were addressed to Orville and had the word "URGENT" printed on them in big letters. He was examining one when Orville reappeared.

"I caught your mom just as she was leaving for home," he announced, "so she should be here any minute."

"Who are these letters from?" Jonas asked, holding up an envelope.

"Those? Fan mail," Orville answered. "Hanging out with the world-famous Crime Cats is rubbing off on me," he laughed weakly. "Come on, we need to get you out of this draft—you're soaked. I'll whip up some hot cocoa."

Soon after Jonas had settled himself before the fire with CatBob and Neil, Mrs. Shurmann came in lugging a large black leather bag. She kissed Jonas on the head and then set to work examining CatBob, who was still out cold.

Jonas helped his mom with the examination, just like he did after school at her veterinary hospital. Midway through the check-up, CatBob jolted awake and startled everyone with a terrible scream.

"I'LL KILL YOU, YOU WHITE—!" he screeched. But the peachy feline paused when his eyes came to focus on Jonas and his mom. "Sorry, Jonas," he muttered. "I thought—"

"Just relax, Buddy." Jonas whispered. "You're safe now." He gently stroked the injured cat's damp coat. "We're back at Castle Dusenbury. My mom's just going to make sure you're all right."

CatBob looked once around the room, then stared straight ahead as if nothing were happening.

"Is he gonna be okay, Mom?" Jonas asked.

"Well," she muttered, "I think he's been in a pretty bad fight, but he should be fine." She smiled up at Jonas. "But someone really rang his fuzzy little bell." She reached down and rubbed Neil's velveteen nose. "You've gotta do a better job of keeping your friend out of trouble," she said teasingly.

"Is she blaming this on me?" Neil asked Jonas. "Because neither Orville or I knew he'd even gotten out."

Orville looked worried. "I hope CatBob's family isn't going to be mad at me," he said. "I don't even know how he got out."

Mrs. Shurmann shook her head. "Considering how many fights he's been in, I doubt they'll even notice." She took off her stethoscope and began replacing all of her instruments in her bag. "He was exhausted more than anything. I'll leave you with some painkillers, but he should be fine in a day or two. Just keep him inside."

Orville turned to Jonas. "Where did you find him, anyway?" he asked.

"In the alley across the street," Jonas said.

Orville's brows knitted. "How did you know to find him *there*?"

"Does your father know you're out?" Mrs. Shurmann asked.

Jonas looked down at the floor. "A bird told me CatBob was in trouble so I went out looking for him."

This drew sidelong glances from Orville and Mrs. Shurmann.

"Uh-*huh*," Jonas's mom said, "I think we're done. Why don't you go get ready—I'm sure your father has some burnt cookies waiting for us." She rubbed Jonas's hair, then snapped her bag shut and went into the kitchen with Orville.

CatBob remained stretched out in front of the fire as Jonas gently stroked his head.

"What were you doing across the street?" Jonas asked, but his friend didn't reply. "You're lucky Phoenix led me to you, otherwise you'd be a cat-cicle right about now." But his friend remained silent and still.

While Orville was thanking Mrs. Shurmann for coming over so quickly, Jonas asked Neil what he thought was going on with CatBob.

"I'm stumped," Neil admitted. "He hasn't answered one question since he became transfixed on that window. I'll try to talk to him, but I don't know how much good it'll do."

Jonas frowned. "Well, *someone* needs to talk to him."

They heard Mrs. Shurmann call from down the

hall and exchanged uneasy goodbyes. Trouble hung in the air like a dark cloud. They were both hoping that things wouldn't seem as bad in the morning, but neither of them could bring themselves to say it aloud. Something just didn't feel right. Deep down they knew this nightmare was only beginning.

4
MAJOR SHURMANN

Chasing the Hooded Figure's car through the neighborhood assured Jonas a long, deep sleep. When he rolled out of bed ten hours later, he felt refreshed and happy. After a bath and breakfast, he suited up and headed out the door with his sled in tow.

Really big snows were rare in Central Ohio and Jonas was determined to make the most of this one before it melted away. Plus, Jonas suspected Orville might need some cheering up after the previous night, so he struck out toward Castle Dusenbury.

Jonas took a big gulp of the crisp air and smiled. The snowstorm had brought with it everything he had hoped for. Massive mounds of snow squatted along the streets where cars had lain buried earlier that morning. As he began scaling the piles, he assumed his secret identity as Major Shurmann of the

Earth Federation Expeditionary Force: the sole survivor of a crash-landing on a frozen alien planet. Jonas reached into his coat pocket and produced his dad's old metal calculator. He pressed a few buttons and made Sci-fi sound effects as he pretended to scan the area. He turned it around and examined the screen. His eyes narrowed. The readings revealed life forms had been detected nearby. He pocketed the calculator and trudged off in the direction indicated in the read out.

His destination was, of course, Orville Dusenbury's house. However, when Major Shurmann reached the doorstep, he found his imaginary instruments had been wrong. Castle Dusenbury stood silent and dark. He rang the doorbell and waited but heard no sound from within. He knocked. Still no answer. Jonas's disappointment was getting very close to ruining his good mood when he heard a muffled chime coming from his coat pocket. Upon retrieving his phone, he discovered a text from Orville.

WHAT R U DOING?

Jonas walked out into the yard and looked up at the dilapidated mansion to see if he could spot his friend watching him from a window, but he couldn't see anyone. He replied.

OUTSIDE FREEZING. LET ME IN.

The reply came immediately:

NOT HOME. MEET ME AT OLD OLENTANGY PARK.

Jonas sighed. The old park was located on Jonas's street just across High. Jonas had walked all the way to Orville's house when his friend had been three blocks away the whole time. Jonas replied.

K LEAVING CASTLE DUSENBURY NOW.

Jonas knew the old park. He had snuck in once with a group of neighborhood kids, but he didn't remember seeing any good sledding spots back there. He decided to leave the sled and try to talk Orville into going sledding later on.

Jonas's dad had taken him sledding a couple of times. Jonas had had so much fun that he figured sledding could cheer anyone up—even Orville. And even though Orville was an adult, and therefore wasn't supposed to enjoy the snow, Jonas knew Orville wasn't really a normal adult. He was usually happy, he didn't complain about things, and Jonas had never noticed him doing many adult things other than working on his house. And even then, Orville wasn't even very good at that. Orville liked to do fun things, like play games and scare the neighborhood kids with his father's medical skeleton—or at least he used to. Lately, however, Orville seemed to be acting more like an adult and something about that worried Jonas.

Orville's street was situated on the side of a hill, like most streets east of High, but Dusenbury was decidedly steeper than most. The walk was slippery and by the third time Jonas's boots went out from under him, he began to regret leaving his sled behind. He could have ridden it all the way to High.

As soon as he reached flat land, he immediately turned and headed south, peeking into shop windows as he went. Jonas loved to browse as he walked. The antique malls were his favorite. The windows were always stuffed with crazy items that Jonas could never imagine anyone buying. Mr. Shurmann had told him that he'd bought Jonas's chicken costume at an antique mall, but Jonas wasn't sure in which one. He slowed to take an extra-careful look in each window he passed, trying to see if he could tell which store it might have been, but none of them appeared to be selling chicken costumes.

Jonas soon spotted a group of kids pulling sleds down the opposite side of the street. He heard one of them call out, "BOCK-BOCK CHICKEN!" Then the kids all waved.

"Hey, Jonas!" one of the boys called. "We're going down to the bike trail to go sledding. Wanna come?" Jonas recognized the voice—it was Danny Martin. Danny was in Miss Keys's class with Jonas and had teased him until Jonas became a local hero.

Since then, Jonas and Danny had become friends.

"I can't," Jonas shouted. "I got a meeting. You going tomorrow?"

"Yeah. I'll text you."

"Cool. See ya." Jonas waved and continued on.

He found the way blocked at the corner of Nightshade Road. Snowplows had pushed a wall of dirty snow and ice as tall as Jonas over the curb and onto the sidewalk. Jonas climbed over the frozen minimountain, only to discover the street on the other side was a pool of water. He turned back around and took the sidewalks up Nightshade to avoid the mess. When he turned the corner back onto High, a familiar group of letters caught his eye: P-H-O-E-N-I-X.

The letters were emblazoned across an Ohio license plate that was bolted to the back of a maroon Volvo station wagon—the very same one Jonas had chased the night before. Jonas blinked. He felt as though he were seeing a ghost in broad daylight. He hadn't expected to see the mysterious car again, much less in the bright sunshine like this. It sat buried in a snowdrift behind a large house that sat on a hill.

The old house loomed over the corner of High Street and Nightshade Road like a giant vulture. Jonas had noticed the place before, but never knew

if it was a business or a private residence. He just remembered it looked spooky like Orville's house. But as he looked at it now, in the sunshine with snow covering its missing shingles and the other rough spots that gave the place its usually foreboding character, it appeared much less threatening.

A wooden sign was crouched under a thicket of withered bushes. A blanket of snow sheltered it from the sun, almost concealing its message from view. The letters painted on the board read PHOENIX BOOKS.

Two flights of crooked stairs climbed to the porch where Jonas saw someone standing behind a glass door. The Hooded Figure reached out with its bony hand and grasped the OPEN sign. With a deft move, the message was changed to CLOSED. Then the specter stepped back and yanked down a blind and was lost from sight.

5
THE PHANTOM'S CALL

Jonas crossed East Thurber at High Street and made his way into a complex of large stone buildings. Mr. Shurmann had once told him that Olentangy Village Apartments had been built in 1940 as part of a pet project of President Franklin D. Roosevelt. The complex even had a bowling alley that Jonas's dad used to go to all the time until it burned down. Enormous birch trees towered among the buildings all around. Their white bark shone in the sunlight like polished marble.

Jonas followed the slushy walkway deeper into the complex before cutting across a parking lot and setting out through the snow. He followed two sets of footprints that led beyond a row of trees and into an empty lot where a lonely bulldozer sat half-buried. On the opposite end, a rusty fence stretched like withered arms around the remaining ruins of an old amusement park. Jonas shuffled up to the crooked gates and slipped through a small gap at the bottom, then continued on his way through the ruins.

The footprints weaved around piles of twisted metal and rotted wood that lay silently under a blanket of snow. Rusted railroad tracks peeked out of the snowdrifts like the spine of a sea monster. Brittle vines clung to the wooden frame and reached up to a sign that had somehow remained standing after decades of neglect. The sign now served more as a grave marker for what was once a ride called THE RED DEVIL.

A little farther along Jonas stopped when he found himself standing in the shadow of a giant cat head that jutted out of the snow. Its gaping mouth was set in a ghoulish grin that served as the entrance to the SCAREDY CAT SPOOK HOUSE, according to the letters that hung askew above its ears. Jonas noticed that the footprints he had been following split into a Y, seemingly to avoid entering the cat's wooden jaws. Jonas peered into the doorway and shivered. Cobwebs waved in the breeze like ghostly hands, beckoning him to enter, but Jonas refused the invitation. He took a step back. It was obvious that the spook house hadn't been safe for humans for many years and he had no desire to find out what sort of creature now made its home in a dark, dangerous place like this.

Jonas followed the footprints around the spook house to the edge of a tree line, where he found Orville Dusenbury talking to a short man with thick glasses. The two men stood in front of an old animal enclosure that was now covered in graffiti. Orville saw him and waved.

"Hey, Jonas! Just hang out for a minute," he called, "we're almost done."

Jonas nodded as he watched Orville usher the man toward the gates. Jonas then shuffled over to a pair of dilapidated buildings that faced the woods. The windowpanes were empty and the walls, like the animal enclosure, had been defaced with spray paint. He leaned into the doorway of the first structure and looked around. The interior walls were covered in more graffiti than the outside. A shabby table sat in the corner on a carpet of broken glass and crushed aluminum cans. The place smelled like a summer camp outhouse—even in the cold. Jonas gagged and backed away.

As he made his way to the next door, he caught a glimpse of a white tail slipping from the space between the buildings. He squeezed through the narrow passage, but found only tiny footprints on the other end.

He followed the tracks around the graffiti-covered buildings and back into the park where they wound through mangled wrecks and crumbling buildings and didn't seem to ever end. And no matter how quickly he ran, Jonas couldn't catch any more than a fleeting glimpse of what he assumed was the tail of a white cat. At least, he thought it was a cat. He wanted it to be, but it seemed to move so fast. Faster than any cat he'd ever seen.

Jonas soon found himself getting tired. His leg muscles and lungs burned from the exertion, forcing him to slow his pace. In fact, he was about to stop when he heard a distant voice call his name. Then something occurred to him. *What if the cat isn't running away? What if it needs my help and is trying to lead me somewhere?* Jonas couldn't stand the thought of giving up if a cat-friend really needed his help.

He heard the voice call to him again.

What if this cat's trying to lead me to kittens that are in danger of freezing? he thought as he stumbled through the snow. Then a parade of terrible scenarios began passing though Jonas's mind. *Maybe it's leading me to another cat that's been injured in a fight or caught in a trap!* He pushed himself to run faster. There was no way he could quit now.

The tracks led into deeper snow, which forced Jonas to lift his legs higher and run faster to keep up his pace. He marched frantically into deeper and deeper drifts. Every time he stumbled and fell, he panicked a little more. Was he going to be able to reach the cat that needed his help in time? It was that very question that allowed him to find the additional strength to leap to his feet and keep moving.

The voice called his name again. It was getting closer.

Ragged edges of rusted steel clawed at his legs and snagged his coat as he climbed through a mess of collapsed bleachers. When he finally emerged on the other side, he found the tracks made a straight line into the trees.

The voice called to him, loud and urgent now.

He broke into a frantic run, mentally readying himself for anything. He balled his fists and gritted his teeth. Maybe he would have to fend off a wild animal, or climb a tree, or put a fire out, or...

As he charged into the wood, his foot caught on a root, sending him tumbling forward. He reached out to stop his fall, but discovered there was nothing to grab onto. The ground disappeared from his vision as he sailed over the edge of a cliff.

6
OLENTANGY PARK

Jonas heard the voice again call his name, but this time it was so close it startled him.

"Jonas, hang on!" Orville shouted. "I've got you!"

Jonas blinked. He suddenly felt disoriented. He felt as though he were floating and when he looked around, he couldn't see Orville. "Orville? What... what's going on?" he called.

"You're going to be fine, Buddy," Orville grunted. "Just do me a favor and don't look down, okay?"

Jonas looked down and saw a creek bed under him. He also noticed that it looked frighteningly small from where he was. He realized that he was hanging in mid-air. A second later, he felt himself moving back toward the edge of the cliff where Orville stood, braced against a tree.

"What's gotten into you?" Orville panted as he lowered Jonas to the ground. "Are you trying to kill yourself?"

Jonas looked around, bewildered. He didn't even know where he was or how he got there. "I don't think so. I mean—no," he said.

"That ravine goes down fifty feet or more," Orville gasped. "If you start to fall, it's impossible to stop yourself. I know because I fell down there."

"You fell down *there?*" Jonas said peering over the edge. "How did you survive?" He turned to find Orville backing away from the edge. His friend was looking at the ground and wringing his hands.

"I don't know," Orville said after a long silence. "I got lucky, I guess." He looked up at Jonas and forced a smile. "I guess that makes two of us." He straightened up and ushered Jonas out of the trees and back toward the park. "Have you ever been back here?" he asked.

"Uh—" Jonas hesitated. He considered what he should admit to. He was pretty sure most every kid in Clintonville had slipped through the gates at one time or another to snoop around the old park, but it was also a well-known fact that the park was a hang-out for teenagers and young kids weren't welcome. "Well, I was with some kids and they—"

Orville broke into a fit of laughter. "Relax,

Drumsticks, I'm not going to rat you out." He slapped Jonas on the back. "I'm pretty sure every kid in Clintonville has been back here at one time or another. Heck, *I* used to screw around back here—and it was *my* family that owned it."

Jonas's eyebrows shot up. "Your family *owns* this place?"

Orville nodded. "Dr. Winslow Dusenbury inherited it from his father and now it's been passed along to me." He turned to face the crumbled ruins that lay half-hidden in the snow. "Believe it or not, this mess was an amusement park at one time."

Jonas gave Orville a sidelong glance. "Seriously?"

"It really was. And not just any amusement park," Orville beamed. "Olentangy Park was the biggest amusement park in America!"

"Seriously?!"

"Yep," Orville nodded. "My great-great-grand-father, John W. Dusenbury and his brother, Will, bought this lot and the land the apartment complex now sits on back in 1899. It was a picnic garden called The Villa when they bought it, but they re-named it Olentangy Park and erected a roller coaster called the Figure Eight. People came from all over to ride the Figure Eight, which allowed the brothers to add all sorts of attractions: a Ferris Wheel, a boathouse, a theater—they bought a Japanese Garden at the 1904 World's Fair and brought it back. Heck! the Dusenburys built Columbus's very first zoo over here and country's largest swimming pool right over there." Orville pointed toward the apartment complex.

"So, what happened?" Jonas asked. "Why did the park close?"

"The Great Depression." Orville said. He smiled ruefully at the remains of his family's legacy. "They ran the park for thirty years. That's quite a run. Then everyone lost their jobs and no one had money to go to an amusement park. John and Will were forced to lease the place to another set of brothers."

Orville's phone rang. He paused to take it out and squinted at the screen. Jonas watched him grimace and then stuff the phone back in his coat. "Ugh!" he grumbled. "Leave me alone, you vampires." Orville turned back to Jonas and smiled. "Now where was I?" he asked.

"Vampires?" Jonas asked.

Orville gave a doubtful look and waved the comment off. "That's nothing," he sniffed. He then turned to face the huge cat head. "*This*," he announced, "was my *favorite* attraction in the park." He walked up and patted the weathered wood. "Of course, I never got to see it when it was operational." He turned to Jonas and winked. "But it was my favorite hang out when I was a kid."

"You used to go in there?" Jonas asked.

Orville's phone rang again. He sighed and pulled it out.

"You can get that if you need to," Jonas offered, but Orville shook his head and shoved the phone back in his coat.

"Anyway," Orville continued. "Oh, man! The Scaredy Cat was my favorite as a kid," Orville exclaimed. "You wanna check it out?"

Jonas looked at the entrance again. The cat's mouth seemed to lead into a black gulf of nothingness. Jonas would have expected anything that passed through the doorway to fall off the face of the Earth. "Uh—" he stammered, trying to think up an excuse as to why he would never—under any circumstances—go in there.

Orville laughed. "You're a smart kid, Drumsticks. I wouldn't go in there for anything now." He clutched his round belly in his mitts and shook it. "I'd probably end up busting through the rickety floor anyway. Then you'd have to call a tow truck to drag me out with a winch."

Jonas relaxed and laughed.

The tour ended back at the ravine. As they approached the trees, Jonas noticed Orville became quiet and nervous again. His smile disappeared and he was wringing his hands. He looked worried.

"I need your help, Jonas," Orville said solemnly. "I need you to help me find something." He looked down at Jonas. His eyes were sad. "Will you help me?"

Orville's grave demeanor took Jonas aback, but he said nothing. He just nodded his head in agreement.

7
BEAST FEAST

Jonas and Orville staggered through the front door of Castle Dusenbury, where Neil Higgins greeted them with a long, deep yawn. He sat atop a floor vent with his feet tucked under him. The cyclopean feline resembled a plump furry chicken warming an egg.

"Really?" Jonas said. "That's all we get—a yawn?"

"I told you, wintertime is tough on cats," Neil said. "The cold makes us lethargic. It's difficult to find the energy to do anything." The gray cat stood up, stretched, and waddled over to the newcomers. "Hello, Jonas," he meowed as he wrapped his tail around Jonas's leg and gave a gentle squeeze. "How's that?"

"That's better," Jonas said with a smile. He kneeled down and showered his friend with pets and scritches.

"Woo! It's good to be inside," Orville exclaimed as he kicked off his boots and tossed the mail down. As soon as he had unwrapped his scarf and shrugged off his coat, he lumbered toward the kitchen. "I'll get some hot cocoa going," he called.

Once Orville was out of sight, Jonas bent down and whispered to his partner."Where's CatBob?" he asked.

Neil shook his head. "He's still at the window. Watching whatever it is he sees out there. I sat for as long as I could, but I couldn't see a thing." The little feline shivered. "The windows in this house are drafty. I could only watch for so long before I had to jump on a vent to warm up."

Jonas frowned. "I wonder what's eating him?" He hung up his coat and began pulling off his boots. "He's not peeing again, is he?"

"Not that I've smelled," Neil whispered. "I kept reminding him not to spray inside."

"Thanks, Buddy, I don't think Orville's mood can take another Pee-Pee Cat episode—"

Jonas stopped. The pair heard the distinct sound of a tin can being peeled open. Neil sprang to attention and took off toward the kitchen shouting, "Beast Feast!"

Jonas shook his head and laughed. He dropped

his dripping boots on the floor vent and hung up his scarf. As he shrugged off his coat he caught sight of the mail Orville had brought in. He picked up one of the envelopes and examined it. The word "UR-GENT" was again printed in bold red letters across the front. They had been thrown onto a pile of identical envelopes Jonas had noticed the night before. He replaced the letter and quietly made his way up the staircase.

He found CatBob sitting on a windowsill at the end of the hall, gazing intently through the frosted panes. Jonas walked up behind the peachy feline and looked out. The window offered a view that spanned the western end of the front yard to the northern edge of the side yard. Jonas stood on his toes and craned his head in an attempt to find what CatBob was watching, but he couldn't see a thing.

Jonas crouched down and stroked his partner's back. CatBob flinched, as if Jonas's presence had surprised him. "Orville and I must be getting sneaky if you didn't hear us come in," Jonas whispered.

CatBob managed to acknowledge Jonas with a weak meow.

"Orville's serving Beast Feast for dinner," Jonas continued quietly. "You'd better claim your bowl before Neil hogs it all."

"Can't eat—working," was all CatBob said.

Jonas ran his hand over CatBob's head, but his partner just looked straight ahead. "Working on what?" Jonas asked.

"Don't worry about it," the peachy feline muttered. "I'll take care of it."

"Take care of what?" Jonas asked, but his partner just continued staring out the window in silence. Jonas frowned. He leaned in and whispered, "That was very inconsiderate to pee-pee in Castle Dusenbury, CatBob!"

CatBob maintained his stony silence.

"Fine. Have it your way," Jonas huffed. He got up and made his way back down the stairs, where he joined Orville and Neil in the kitchen. Orville greeted him with a steaming mug of cocoa, but before he took it, Jonas snapped up CatBob's bowl off the floor and set it on the counter.

"Hey, if CatBob won't eat it, let Neil have it," Orville said coolly.

"Yes, let *me* have it," Neil cried between gulps. "I'm almost finished with mine."

"He'll eventually get hungry," Jonas said, "and if you think pee-pee's no fun to clean up, you'll be in for a nasty surprise when you stuff Neil full of wet food. It will only be a matter of time before the Beast Feast Bomb goes off—all over the place."

Orville chuckled and placed the bowl in the

43

refrigerator. Then, he handed Jonas both mugs of cocoa and led him upstairs to a closed door. There, he reached into his sweater pocket and produced a tarnished skeleton key.

Jonas had been helping Orville clean his house for a couple of months and had never once known him to lock any doors aside from the front and back entrances. Orville grabbed the doorknob with his other hand and twisted the key. "Voila!" he exclaimed, but nothing happened. "Huh," he muttered, "the lock must be stuck."

"What *is* this room?" Jonas asked.

"This will be my study one day," he said as he jiggled the key in the lock. "But for now," he braced himself against the door and gripped the key with both hands, "this room is..."

The key turned with a loud *klack-klack*! The door creaked open and Orville flipped a switch. "Ta-da!" he sang as he grabbed his mug of cocoa.

A single light bulb sputtered to life, revealing... a mess. An enormous mess. In fact, this was by far the messiest room Jonas had seen in Orville's house. It was packed from wall to wall with stack upon stack of... *stuff*. Furniture, boxes, books, clothes, cans, doors, fixtures, records, magazines, toys—you name it. All dusty, all dirty, and all forgotten about until now. Some of the piles were as tall as Jonas and a few stacks towered well over the ends of Orville's Afro.

"Holy crap!" Jonas exclaimed.

Orville laughed weakly. "Yeah, it's a mess, huh?"

"Oh man, I don't think I have the energy to clean after running in the park," Jonas said.

"We're not here to clean, Drumsticks," Orville said. "Actually, I expect we'll make the mess even worse than it is." He waded over to a ladder that was set up in the middle of the room and switched on a rack of work lights that were mounted to one of the rungs. Then he picked up a small box and opened it. "We're here to find a document—a very important document. One that I'm certain is in this room. And we need to find it soon."

"How do you know it's in here?" Jonas asked.

"Well, it's a very important document, so I did what any responsible person would do: I put it someplace *safe*. But now I can't remember where that someplace safe was, *exactly*." He set the box down and picked up another. "I've looked everyplace else, hoping it would be in another room, but no luck—it has to be in *this* room."

8
SOMETHING MISSING

"Okay," Jonas said, "what's this document look like?"

"You can't miss it." Orville opened the box in his hands and sifted through the contents. "It's got the words UNITED STATES OF AMERICA printed in big, fancy letters at the top."

Jonas nodded. He repeated the description under his breath as he began opening boxes. The pair worked in silence for a solid hour, only speaking to say *Gesundheit* when the other caught a nose full of dust and sneezed.

Orville worked with a quiet determination that Jonas had never seen before. Usually his friend never stopped talking. He was always busy cracking jokes or telling stories, but lately Orville just didn't seem himself. Jonas was silent for other reasons. He had been trying to decide on the best way to apologize to Orville for CatBob peeing in the house. But so far he had failed to think of a clever way to bring it up. Every time he started a conversation he got nervous and fell silent again. After a few false starts, he finally decided to just say it. "I just want you to know..." he stammered.

Orville grunted and continued working.

"Well, Neil and I feel really bad about CatBob peeing in Castle Dusenbury," he said weakly, "and we want you to know we're sorry." He paused, waiting for an acknowledgement.

"Uh-huh," Orville grunted.

Jonas grabbed another box and sifted through the contents absentmindedly. He waited for Orville to say more, but his friend just kept working. Jonas couldn't tell if Orville had actually heard him, or if he had been too preoccupied searching. He paused again and said, "I just wanted you to know we're sorry."

"You're sorry," Orville grumbled as he flung a box to the floor, "I get it." The crashing sound startled Jonas.

Jonas felt a cold sweat break out on his forehead. Even though weird things had been happening over the previous two days, he hadn't really been scared until that moment. Orville Dusenbury was one of his best friends and the happiest guy he knew. And above all else, Orville loved the neighborhood cats—especially CatBob and Neil—but something must have been seriously wrong for Orville to dismiss Jonas's apology and stay angry at CatBob. Jonas had never seen Orville like this. He didn't seem like the same person.

A series of hisses and screams came spilling in from the hall. "Quiet down!" Orville called. He huffed and shook his head, then he motioned to Jonas. "Hey, Jonas," he called, "come here and help me with this, would you?"

Jonas ferreted his way through the wreckage to where Orville was clearing space in front of the tallest stack in the room.

"Just try and keep this chair steady for me," Orville said as he stepped on it. He reached over his head and shifted a large box at the top of the stack. He sucked in his breath as the package came to rest on the very tips of his fingers. He took a slow step down. "There we go," he said in a strained whisper.

That's when a jarring scream echoed in from the hall, followed by a crash. Orville's head instinctively snapped toward the commotion and the weight over his head shifted.

"No, no, no, no!" he cried as his grip was lost and the box came crashing down. It tumbled into a smaller stack and sent junk spilling across the floor.

Neil came skittering through the doorway, his ears and tail standing at attention. "Come quick, Jonas—it's CatBob!"

Jonas glanced up at Orville, whose eyes looked as though they were about to escape his head. His chest was heaving and his hands were knotted into shaking fists. Jonas had never seen a volcano erupt in person, but he imagined it would look like Orville did at that moment. "Please don't hurt CatBob," Jonas pleaded.

"Jonas," Orville said in a shaking whisper, "you'd better get that crazy cat before I do." He gritted his teeth as he began to growl, "because I don't know what I'll do if I get my hands on him!"

9
WARNING

Jonas and Neil rushed to the end of the hallway where they found the floor covered in shattered glass. The curtain twisted in a stiff wind that blew through the broken panes. Jonas glanced around the room, but there was no sign of CatBob. He carefully stepped to the window and leaned out. There, he found his peachy partner on the roof, back arched and hackles raised, hissing at something in the yard below.

Jonas could hear Orville's voice getting closer. He frantically called to his feline friend to come inside. When CatBob turned to face him, his paws slipped out from under him, sending the cat sliding backward until he disappeared from view. Jonas wailed. All he could see was two blonde paws clinging to a small chunk of ice attached to one of the slate shingles. He shouted to his friend to hold on and ducked back inside.

Jonas bolted back down the hall, past Orville who had just discovered the shattered window. He darted into the study and snatched the extension cord connected to the work lights. He yanked it from the outlet and came scrambling back down the hall. Jonas wrapped one end of the cord around his waist and shouted to Orville to grab the other and get ready.

Orville was still glaring at the glass shards on the floor. "Ready for what?!" he snapped.

"Grab the cord or we're both gonna die!" Jonas yelled as he dove headfirst through the window and onto the roof.

Orville managed to bend down and snatch the cord just before it went taut. He braced himself against the wall and paused. "You still there?" he called through the window.

"Still here!" Jonas shouted back. "Both of us."

Jonas had managed to grab CatBob just as the ice he'd been clinging to gave way. But even though the peachy feline had escaped the fall, he continued hissing and screaming at something below. As the pair slowly spun in the breeze, Jonas scanned the yard for CatBob's enemy. He didn't see anything move, but he did notice many sets of animal tracks winding all over the yard. They all seemed to converge on a tree that grew beside the house, and Jonas noticed the snow on many of the branches had been trampled.

Orville wrapped some of the cord around his hands and called out. "Here we go. Just hold still, okay?" Then he began reeling in the cord with even, gentle motions.

It was then that Jonas spied something in the yard—or more specifically, some*one*. A familiar shape slipped out of the shadows of the feral hedges that lined the yard. Jonas gasped. The Hooded Figure looked up at him, and then quickly turned and crept away.

"Pull us up—quick!" Jonas yelled. "Hurry up!"

Orville winced and huffed as his precious cargo emerged from the edge of the roof. With a few more pulls, Jonas came clambering through the window, dragging in snow, and shouting. He dropped CatBob on the floor and took off down the hall. He leaped down the stairs and began jamming himself into his snow gear, or at least most of it. As soon as his boots and coat were on, he dashed out the door.

At the edge of the yard, he discovered fresh footprints and followed them down Dusenbury Street and around the corner to Moors Avenue. As soon as he rounded the bend he saw the maroon station wagon idling on the side of the street. Frozen clouds of exhaust puffed from the tail pipe as the car prepared to escape. Jonas ran to the driver's side door and pressed his face to the window in an attempt to identify the Figure, but the person inside was breathing on the window. All Jonas could see was the fog on the glass. He had been outsmarted.

Jonas pounded on the window with his fists. "Who are you?" he shouted.

There was no answer. The engine revved and Jonas stepped away to let the car go. But to his surprise, it didn't move. Instead, he saw a finger cut a line through the window fog. A message began to form. Jonas breathed the words as he read them:

PHANTOM
STRIKES
TONIGHT

When the message was finished, the car roared off around the bend.

Jonas returned to a somber scene at Castle Dusenbury. Neil hid under a cabinet and CatBob sulked in a corner while Orville picked up shards of glass and tossed them into a bucket. No one said a word. Jonas grabbed a broom and dustpan and silently joined Orville in the cleanup. After the floor had been cleared, they set to work taping a plastic sheet over the broken window. When the job was finished, Orville muttered his thanks and lumbered downstairs to the kitchen. Jonas called his dad and told him that he and his friends needed to be picked up right away. He'd just finished loading Neil into his cat carrier and went to pick up CatBob, when the peach feline suddenly lashed out. The strike left a long, red line down Jonas's forearm.

"Ow!" Jonas yelped. "What's wrong with you?!"

"I can't go," CatBob said as he backed away. "Orville needs me here. I told you I'd take care of it, so just let me go."

"And some job you did," Jonas hissed. "Thanks to you, Orville doesn't want any of us here anymore and I don't blame him. You're acting crazy."

"I'm not crazy," CatBob growled. "I'm sorry, Jonas, I didn't mean to hurt you. I just have to take care of this."

"Uh-oh! Too late," Jonas said as straightened up, "Looks like Orville's going to take care of you himself." CatBob turned to face Orville, but found the hallway empty. Jonas reached down and hauled his friend up by the scruff, tossing him into his carrier and zipping it up.

"You tricked me!" CatBob hissed. "Let me out right now!"

"No way," Jonas grumbled as he examined the blood rising on his skin. "Way to show your appreciation to the guy who saved your life, Jerk!"

10
THE
THING
IN THE
TUNNEL

Jonas slept with Neil Higgins curled up at his feet, while CatBob stood vigil at Jonas's bedroom window, watching, waiting, for *something*.

Only a few blocks away, Orville Dusenbury emerged from his future study at 10:45 PM. He was covered from head to toe in dust and grime, but the layer of filth only served to accentuate the thousand-watt smile shining from beneath his beard. He staggered out of the avalanche waving a rolled-up paper in his hand. He snaked his way to the door and leaped into the hallway, boogieing like a madman. He shook his hips down the hall while singing in a high falsetto voice, "Yeah! Uh-huh! Heavy Metal Pizza! Oh, yeah! Uh-huh! Heavy Metal Pizza Time!"

He stopped at the top of the stairs and suddenly took on a grave expression. Then he spread his arms wide and announced to the empty house, "Brothers and sisters! The time has come!" He shimmied down the stairs while shouting, "Oh, yes, mamma! The time has come! For sauce and cheese so HOT, they will melt your FACE!"

He strutted down the hall, flapping his arms in a comical Chicken Walk. He bobbed his head all the way to the kitchen, where he stopped and belted, "The time has come for a sweet, delicious... HEAVY METAL SPECIAL!" The last bit he screeched at the top of his lungs while contorting his face in mock agony.

He took out his phone and called Gatto's Pizza. He placed an order for a pepperoni pie and an Italian sub—his usual order. Orville was so famished from his search that before he'd even replaced the phone in his pocket, he began imagining the aromas of Italian spices, cooked meats, and melted cheeses. His mouth watered in anticipation. And this meal was sure to be especially delicious because Orville was celebrating a victory.

But for Orville Dusenbury, Pizza Night was just as much about the *ritual* as it was about the food. Gatto's was the oldest pizza place in Clintonville. In fact, the shop was presently operating in the same location it had on the day it opened in 1952. But its history wasn't the reason Orville loved Gatto's. It was because Gatto's was responsible for inspiring his unlikely love affair with Heavy Metal music.

That love began when he'd decided to treat himself to a homecoming feast his first night back in Clintonville a few years ago. Thirty minutes after phoning in his order, a roar of screeching guitars drew him outside to investigate. He discovered the unholy racket was coming from the Gatto's delivery car. Orville ran out to pay and returned happy, hungry, and half-deaf, with his large pepperoni pizza and Italian sub.

Needless to say, that first pizza was so delicious that Orville had been a loyal customer ever since. But the experience had an unexpected consequence: Orville found himself suffering mighty cravings for pizza any time he heard Heavy Metal. His brain had formed a direct connection between the taste of pizza and the music he'd heard when he received it. Since then, Orville preferred to spend the delivery time whetting his appetite in the loudest way possible.

Orville swaggered over to a shelf stuffed with LPs and selected an album. He unsheathed the record and gently dropped it onto the turntable. He cued up the needle and shouted as if addressing an arena full of screaming fans, "Castle Dusenbury! Are you ready to SCREAM FOR PIZZA?!" The needle met the vinyl and ignited an explosion of sound.

Orville was instantly lost in a deafening frenzy of buzzsaw guitar solos, pepperoni, ham, and cheese.

Two hours later, Orville was passed out in his recliner with a pizza box resting on his chest. The food had satisfied his hunger, but it had also stirred his dreams, as late-night meals often do. Orville didn't know it, but something had happened earlier that day that had caused a long-forgotten memory to resurface. Something he had buried in his mind a long time ago. Something that had scared him. Something he didn't quite understand.

Orville woke up in the dry creek bed at the bottom of a ravine—the one by the park. He winced as he staggered to his feet. Sharp pain shot from his feet up his leg. He looked around for a way out. That's when he discovered the mouth of a large tunnel looming behind him. Strange sounds rattled out of the murky depths. Then a pair of eyes blinked open in the black gulf and a terrible scream echoed through the ravine. Orville let out a cry and hobbled away as fast he could. He clambered up the ravine wall in a panicked frenzy, only pausing to glance over his shoulder. That's when he saw the Thing in the Tunnel had crawled from darkness and was creeping toward the ravine wall— toward him.

Orville clawed at the dirt, grasped at roots, and heaved himself upward by the bark of the trees. But every time he looked over his shoulder, the Thing in the Tunnel drew closer. Pain jolted through him as loose soil gave under his step, but he dared not rest. For no matter how high he climbed, or how fast he scrambled, the Thing in the Tunnel was gaining on him. He climbed frantically, crying, screaming, calling out for help, but there was no one to hear him. He had snuck into the park. No one knew he was there—all alone, being chased by the Thing in the Tunnel.

Orville reached the cliff's edge and stumbled out of the trees. He mounted his bicycle and began pedaling as fast as he could, but when he glanced back, he found the Thing in the Tunnel was right behind him. It scratched at his ankles and its terrible cries echoed in his head all the way home.

When he arrived home, Orville's father demanded to know where he'd been. Orville admitted he'd snuck into the park and had fallen into the ravine. Dr. Dusenbury was furious. He scolded Orville and forbade him to enter the park again. But when Orville told his father about the Thing in the Tunnel, Dr. Dusenbury suddenly fell silent. And that was the scariest thing of all. That was the first time Orville had seen fear in his father's face.

That night, Orville was haunted by nightmares. Every time he tried to go to sleep he would see the Thing's glowing eyes blink open in the blackness, jolting him awake. Orville rolled out of bed. As he shuffled toward the bathroom, he noticed a figure seated at the window at the end of the hall. The person sat still in the moonlight at the same window CatBob had been guarding.

Orville slowly approached the figure. It was his father. Every night, for the following two weeks, Dr. Winslow Dusenbury sat at that same window, watching, waiting, for something—but what? Finally, one night, Orville shuffled over and tugged on his father's sleeve. "What are you waiting for, Sir?" he asked. His father turned to him and Orville saw his head was that of a giant, white cat.

"For you, of course!" the cat screeched.

11
THE PHANTOM STRIKES!

Orville jolted awake. He coughed. He felt as though something heavy was sitting on his chest, making it difficult to breathe. His first thought was that he was having a heart attack, but then the curious sound of lips smacking caught his attention. He peered down at his chest and was met by a fuzzy face. A gray cat as round as a watermelon was standing on his chest, nibbling at one of the remaining pizza squares in the greasy box.

"Who—" he said haltingly as he shifted in his chair. "How did you—"

The startled feline leaped onto the floor and scurried into the hall. Orville sat up and looked around. He was sitting in the study. The boxes of family photos he had been perusing were where he'd left them, but something was missing. He flung himself from the chair and tossed the pizza box aside. Where was the rolled-up document? He'd brought it up and now it was gone. And how did that cat—

Orville walked into the hallway and stopped in his tracks. Twenty cats sat silently watching him in the moonlight.

"If CatBob and Neil told you there was a party here, they lied," he announced. "You missed it—the pizza's all gone!"

Orville noticed a flapping sound coming from the window at the end of the hall. The plastic sheet he had taped up now hung in shreds. It was then that he knew his feline visitors had broken into his home.

Then something appeared that took his breath away. A *terrible* vision. Something Orville hadn't seen since the day he tumbled down the ravine. A large white cat emerged from around the corner. Had Orville never seen the animal before, he would have assumed by its size that it was a dog. But there in the hall, there was no mistaking its feline lineage. And there was no mistaking the fact he had indeed seen it before. Orville shivered. He clasped his hands together and began wringing them. It was the Thing in the Tunnel, in the flesh, standing before him, there in his house, after twenty years—holding his rolled-up document in its teeth.

"Wait!" he stammered. "St— stop! That's mine.

He took a step toward the window and the cats came alive, arching their backs and hissing at him in unison. He paused.

With a silent, graceful leap, the giant white cat passed through the hole in the plastic sheet, with the other cats following closely behind. In a moment, Orville was alone again. He ran to the window and watched as the cats vanished into the wild hedgerow at the edge of the yard.

His stomach suddenly felt queasy. His legs wobbled under his weight. Orville sank to the floor and buried his face in his hands. Deep, wrenching sobs spasmed through his body. He cried uncontrollably for a whole hour, before his grief overwhelmed him completely and delivered him to a deep sleep.

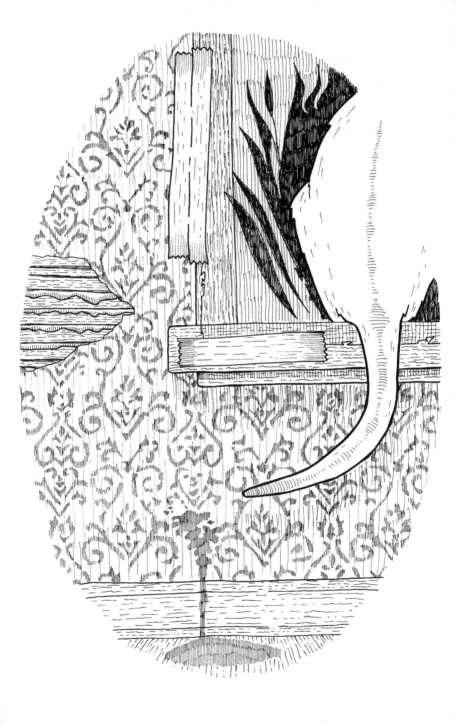

12
IN THE PHANTOM'S WAKE

Jonas brought dishes of food and water to his bedroom window, where CatBob was still keeping his vigil. He examined the floor under the window and was relieved to find it dry. He tried to talk to his peachy partner, but CatBob remained silent, so Jonas took Neil downstairs to join his parents for breakfast.

The Shurmanns were making plans to visit the Clintonville Community Market while they worked through the tall stack of hot fluffy pancakes Jonas's dad had cooked. Jonas and his mom were insisting a trip to the movie theater was in order when the kitchen phone rang.

"Another sales call," Mr. Shurmann grumbled. "I'll get it." He lumbered over and snapped the receiver off its mount. A moment later, he was holding the phone out to Jonas. "For you," he said.

Jonas slid out of his seat and took the phone. "Hello," he said. Orville was on the other end and he sounded strange. He said he needed Jonas to come over as soon as he could, that it was an emergency. Jonas told him he would come over right after breakfast and hung up.

Jonas's parents looked concerned. "Is everything okay?" Mr. Shurmann asked.

Jonas shrugged. "I don't think so. That was Orville." He crept back into his chair and lifted his fork. "Sounds like he really needs my help."

"Okay," Mr. Shurmann nodded. "I guess I can drop you off. I'm going that way anyway."

Jonas and Neil arrived at Castle Dusenbury an hour later. The two detectives found Orville in a terrible state. His clothes were wrinkled and dirty and the toothy grin he usually wore had been replaced by a frown. His brows were knitted with worry and his eyes were bloodshot and swollen from crying. As soon as they entered the house, Orville proceeded to bombard them with his story of finding the deed, ordering a Heavy Metal Special, then waking up to a cat invasion. Jonas sat with Neil on his lap, translating Orville's story in the feline's ear.

Orville was beside himself with worry. "I think I might be going crazy," he gasped, "but I can't remember anything else that could explain the disappearance. And if I don't get that document back I'm going to be homeless."

"Homeless?" Jonas asked. "What do you mean? What's so important about that document, anyway?"

"It's the land deed," Orville said, "to the acres that the ruins of Olentangy Park sit on. That was the buyer you saw me talking to yesterday. He's planning to build a grocery store there and he's prepared to pay me a lot of money for the land."

"But if you own the land, you can still sell it to him, right?"

Orville shook his head. "Although the land has been owned by my family for over a hundred years, without the actual deed, I'm not the owner." He flopped down in a chair and rubbed his forehead. "According to Ohio law, 'he who possesses the deed owns the land.'"

Jonas and Neil exchanged worried glances. "So," Jonas said carefully, "according to the law, a large white cat now owns the land?"

"That's right," Orville said. "And without the money from the sale, I'm going to lose Castle Dusenbury. My pile of 'fan mail' in the front hall is foreclosure notices from the bank." He leaned over, looking down at the floor as if he expected the solution to his problems to skitter out from under the furniture like an insect. "I mean, that story sounds crazy, right? It couldn't have happened." He paused while he fidgeted with the belt of his bathrobe. "But if I am sure I'm remembering things right and it *did* happen, I don't know what to do. I can't go to the police. They'll think I'm a kook!" He wrung his hands. "And who knows where that white cat ran off to?"

Jonas leaned over to Neil and nodded as the feline spoke into his ear. "Neil wants to know if you've ever seen that big white cat before," Jonas said.

Orville looked across the room, as if he was studying something on the far wall, but Jonas knew he was actually watching something in his mind. After a long pause, Orville muttered, "No."

Jonas and Neil exchanged glances again. Something wasn't right.

Jonas placed Neil on the floor and stood up. "Well, we're not gonna solve this mystery by sitting here all day." He grabbed Orville's arm and pulled him up. "First thing we need to do is get this place put back together."

Orville nodded.

The cats had ransacked the downstairs in their search for the deed and Jonas had learned from his dad that a messy house never helps a bad mood. Any time Jonas was feeling down, the first thing his dad told him to do was clean his room. Although that was never what he wanted to hear, it never failed to make him feel better and able to think more clearly.

After two hours of cleaning, the house was back to being what Orville referred to as "organized chaos." Jonas called up Gatto's while Orville cleaned himself up. By the time he made it back downstairs, Jonas had another Heavy Metal Special laid out for him in the kitchen. Orville even managed to crack a smile.

13
SCAREDY CATS

Jonas and Neil were surprised when their news of the theft broke CatBob's silence.

"We need to find that white cat—and fast," Cat-Bob exclaimed. "Does Orville know where it lives?"

"I'm afraid not, Bob," Neil said. "We found tracks in the yard left by twenty different cats—and one of them quite large—but we could only follow them as far as the sidewalk. Beyond the yard the tracks were trampled by people and cars," he added. "Who knows where they're hiding!"

"I think I know," Jonas said.

Jonas, CatBob, and Neil trudged across North High Street and made their way back to the park gates. A Saturday night party was under way in the building facing the ruins and the sounds of music and laughter echoed across the empty lot like ghosts. It was weird to Jonas to see that happy times were unfolding so close to a place where sadness seemed to hang in the air.

The trio quietly slipped through the gates. The snow reflected enough moonlight that a flashlight was unnecessary. But the glow only added to the creepy atmosphere. Each of the detectives felt as though someone or some*thing* was watching them. Neil was always paranoid about things *getting* him and claimed being *got* was every cat's worst fear. While Jonas was often amused by feline paranoia, he presently found himself dealing with the same fear as they crept along.

The detectives eventually found themselves at the entrance of the Scaredy Cat Spook House. The maniacal grin of the feline façade sent chills down Jonas's spine. It didn't look comical or fun looming before him in the moonlight. It looked evil, like a giant wooden predator that had found its next meal in him and his companions.

CatBob crouched and let out a low growl. Neil and Jonas spun around to face their friend and discovered they had been surrounded. The hackles raised on CatBob's back as he whined a high-pitched warning to the feline figures that were emerging from the shadows all around them. There were cats of all kinds: shorthaired, longhaired, tabbies, cow cats, calico, all closing in fast. Hisses and whines were exchanged until a voice from above brought a sudden silence to the scene.

"You are trespassers on private property!" the voice boomed.

Jonas looked up to see the biggest cat he'd ever seen perched on top of the Spook House entrance. "No, we aren't," he shouted back at the white feline. "Orville Dusenbury owns this land and he gave us permission to be here. *You're* trespassing!"

The cats stared at Jonas for a few moments. Even the White Phantom narrowed its blue eyes, studying him. Then the moment passed and the cats continued to close in on the detectives.

"Halt!" the Phantom screeched. The encroaching felines froze in their tracks. "Since you can understand me, listen very carefully, boy. Orville Dusenbury does *not* own this land. This park is the legal property of the Glen Echo Destruction. And any friend of a Dusenbury is not welcome in *our* home." The white cat puffed its chest triumphantly. "You must leave—now!"

"Leave!" the other cats hissed.

CatBob leaped forward and swung wildly at the clowder. The cats in his path ducked and scrambled away from his flying paws. Jonas snatched the peachy feline up and held him tight. "Cool it!" he hissed through gritted teeth.

"The land deed isn't yours," Jonas called to the Phantom as he struggled to keep hold of his squirming partner. "You stole it last night and we're here to demand its return."

The White Cat howled with laughter. "The Dusenburys don't make demands anymore. Their reign of terror is over." The Phantom's jaws snapped with every word, as if it were biting at an invisible enemy. "Our home cannot be taken away, not even by that monster, Orville, or the machines he sends to our gates!"

The cats pushed in closer, forcing the trio against the doorway. CatBob growled protests under the slippery sleeves of Jonas's coat.

"Orville isn't a monster!" Jonas shouted. "He's the nicest guy I know, and he's a friend to all cats!"

"Do you hear that?" the Phantom howled. "Orville Dusenbury sent the machines to scare us because he's our *friend*." The giant feline snorted. "Your ignorance disgusts me, child."

CatBob wiggled out from under Jonas's arms and dropped to the snow growling and hissing. He lunged into the crowd of cats and delivered a flurry of blows. The battered felines screeched and retreated. "Bring your worthless hide down here, Snowflake!"

CatBob shouted. "We'll settle this right now."

"Get ready to run," Jonas whispered to Neil as he scooped up a pile of snow in his arms. He leaped forward and flung it at the gathering cats. The felines backed away momentarily, but as soon as they recovered, Jonas began kicking snow into their faces. He snatched up CatBob and took off toward the gates with Neil following at his heels.

The detectives weaved their way around the buried wrecks and reached the gates, only to find themselves surrounded again. Feline forms seemed to pour from every foul, shadowy nook in the park. Jonas tossed CatBob down and ushered him through the gates. The trio broke into a mad dash toward the apartment complex. Jonas glanced back and saw the feline army had not only followed them beyond the gates, but were closing in fast. At the speed they were running, Jonas knew he and his friends would be lucky to reach the parking lot before the angry horde overtook them.

"No, no, no!" he heard Neil cry. Jonas looked to his side and saw a large, mackerel-striped tabby swiping at Neil's butt. Jonas drifted beside Neil's pursuer and kicked a heap of snow into the cat's face. The tabby tumbled into a drift and disappeared from sight. Jonas turned his attention back to the parking lot ahead where a bright flash of light burst from the darkness. He squinted and saw a car skid to a halt at the end of the footpath.

"Run for that car!" he yelled to his partners. Jonas wasn't sure who was in the car, but his gut told him it was there for them.

"That car better not *get* me," Neil gasped.

As they neared, the passenger side door swung open and the dome light flickered on. The Hooded Figure extended a gloved hand that beckoned them to enter.

"Oh, no!" Jonas gasped.

CatBob and Neil were already leaping into the vehicle. Jonas wanted to tell them to get out, but the nip of claws at his legs left him no choice. He held his breath, dove into the seat, and swung the door closed behind him. He looked up to see the windshield covered with paw pads and hissing faces. The Hooded Figure pounded on the steering wheel. The car's horn blasted through the parking lot, startling a few of the fuzzy attackers from the windshield. But others stayed, clawing at the glass and screeching. The Figure flipped a lever on the steering column and the windshield wiper blades sprang to life, shooing the remaining felines away.

"Hold on," a voice shouted from under the hood. The engine revved. The car lurched forward. The trio was thrown back into their seats as the car roared off through the snow.

Jonas was tempted to steal a glance under the hood, but he was too busy trying to comfort his frightened partners. CatBob and Neil were shaken from the chase and were presently panicked by being in a moving car. Neil had explained to Jonas that cats always need to be in control of their surroundings, and since cats couldn't drive cars, riding in them was scary. So it was no surprise that the two detectives had piled onto Jonas's lap and were meowing their alarm. When the station wagon finally jolted to a stop, the cats both sighed with relief and jumped down onto the seat.

"Come with me," the Figure commanded as it stepped out into the frigid night.

The trio crept out of the car and looked around. The hulking silhouette of Phoenix Books loomed above them in the moonlight. The Hooded Figure stood holding a door open.

"It reminds me of Castle Dusenbury," Jonas whispered nervously. "I— I *think* it's okay, guys. If this person wanted to hurt us, they would have let those cats get us."

His friends nodded in agreement. The detectives stepped past the Hooded Figure and into the darkened doorway.

14
PHOENIX BOOKS

Jonas, CatBob, and Neil reached the top of a long stairwell and were led into a dark room. The detectives stood still, listening to the Hooded Figure's robe rustling in the gloom. Then a match was struck and a yellow flame sizzled to life. The detectives heard the crackle of fire and smelled the scent of smoke. They stepped back as the Figure rose from the glowing hearth and disappeared into a darkened corner of the room.

"Wait here and make yourselves at home," the Figure called. The floor creaked under their host's steps and the detectives heard a door close behind them. Footfalls faded away to another end of the house. The trio was alone.

Jonas's teeth chattered uncontrollably, partly from the cold and partly from fear. He huddled close to the fire and hugged himself tightly. Within a few minutes, the fire bloomed and the room was awash in a cozy glow. Better yet, Jonas's teeth stopped clacking together. He peeled out of his boots and coat while his partners stretched out to soak up the fire's heat and aroma.

Jonas glanced around the room. "See, this isn't so bad—huh, guys?" he said unsteadily.

Indeed, the room looked tidy by the firelight. Old photos hung on the walls and a big bookshelf stood to the right. The house really did remind Jonas of Castle Dusenbury, except this place wasn't a disaster area.

CatBob and Neil raised their heads and sniffed the air. Then the felines stared wide-eyed at something just behind Jonas. Jonas swung around to discover the Hooded Figure looming over him, clutching a metal tray. Jonas screamed and leaped to his feet.

"Stay behind me, guys!" Jonas shouted, "I'll save you from—"

"Calm down—Jeez!" the Hooded Figure commanded.

Jonas blinked. He stood awkwardly, not knowing what to do with himself.

"Now, take the two dishes off the tray and set them on the floor," the Figure continued.

Jonas reached out and lifted the two white dishes

with trembling hands. He crouched down and set them on the floor. His partners rushed to the plates. Jonas saw the dishes were filled with wet food.

"...From... Beast Feast?" Jonas muttered. He turned to find the Hooded Figure was already seated in a high-backed chair gripping a steaming mug in its hands.

The Figure motioned for Jonas to take the other high-backed chair.

He found a matching mug awaiting him beside his chair. He cautiously lifted it and sniffed the contents. It was hot cocoa and it smelled delicious. He looked down at his friends who were greedily devouring their Beast Feast. Jonas shrugged his shoulders and took a sip. It tasted as good as it smelled.

The Figure replaced its mug on a stand and peeled back its hood.

15
UNDER THE HOOD

The black hood fell back and a mane of long, black hair spilled forward. The hair shimmered in the firelight. A woman's smiling face peeked out from behind the flowing strands. The woman giggled when she saw the surprised expression on Jonas's face.

"You— You're..." Jonas stammered.

"A woman?" she asked.

"Human!" Jonas breathed.

"Well, duh! Of course I'm *human*." The woman snorted a laugh. "What did you expect?"

Jonas didn't answer; he just stared at her in amazement.

Her brows rose as she took a sip from her mug. "No, seriously—what *did* you expect me to be?"

"I... I guess I..." Jonas stammered haltingly.

"Did you expect to find my robe was empty

inside?" she asked. "Were you expecting me to be a wraith that haunted the book store and saved you and your friends from a stampede of feral cats in my otherworldly station wagon?"

"I guess not—" Jonas began.

"Because that's what I've been pretending to be," the woman cut in excitedly. "I mean, I'm not *really* a ghost, of course, but all of this sneaking around and hiding in the shadows has been super-fun and I guess I've been getting a little carried away."

Jonas raised his eyebrows.

The woman snorted another laugh and extended her hand. "I'm Lula Kobayashi. Well, *Tallula*, actually. My friends call me Lu-Ko, except for my sister—she calls me Ta-Ko—but, whatever, she's the only person that's allowed to call me that. I'm a *human* girl, and Phoenix Books is my store *and* my home."

"I'm Jonas Shurmann," Jonas muttered as he shook her hand, "and these are my friends, CatBob and Neil Higgins. Thanks for saving us." He looked sidelong at her. "So, you've been sneaking around and spying on us? Is that how you knew we were in the park?"

"Well," Tallula smiled ruefully, "I *might* have been sort of spying on you since I found CatBob in the alley. When I read his tag I knew who he was because of the newspaper story last fall, but I didn't really want to get involved, so I just tried to lead you to him."

She took a long drink and wiped her mouth with the sleeve of her robe. "After that, I thought you guys might need someone watching your back, and since I don't sleep much and I get *really* bored through the winter..." Tallula winced as if she was anticipating something striking her at any moment. "...Well, you guys are, like, my new hobby."

Jonas stared down at the floor, considering this revelation.

"Sorry," she added. "I know spying on you guys is weird and creepy, but you're famous detectives and I'm... not. I just wanted to help."

"It's all right. We're lucky you followed us tonight," Jonas said. "If you hadn't been there to save us, who knows what would have happened. Thank you."

Tallula smiled. "I'm glad I could help. I had a feeling you guys might need some assistance. The White Phantom is more than just a cat—that's for sure!"

"That big white cat?" Jonas asked. "Is that the White Phantom you've been warning me about?"

CatBob and Neil sauntered over to Jonas and hugged his legs with their tails.

"So, is she okay?" CatBob asked.

"Yeah, she's a friend," Jonas answered. "Guys, say hello to Tallula."

The felines circled Tallula's chair, arching their backs and meowing greetings. She cooed compliments as she stroked their backs and rubbed their velvety noses. After a few minutes, Jonas's partners were satisfied and settled down in front of the fire to join the conversation. Jonas climbed down from his chair and took a spot on the rug between them to translate.

Tallula began, "The White Phantom has lived in Olentangy Park for over a hundred years."

"Dogwash!" Neil exclaimed. "The oldest cat ever recorded was Creme Puff, who lived to 38 calendar years and three days."

Tallula paused and waited for Jonas to translate his feline friend's outburst. Once he had, Tallula gave him a suspicious look. "You're not making this up, are you?" she asked. "Did he *really* say that?"

Jonas continued translating to his partner in a hushed voice. The cyclopean feline waddled over to Tallula and meowed while tapping her leg with his paw. She leaned over and asked Jonas what his friend was saying now.

"He says he absolutely *did* say that and it's a fact whether you believe it or not," Jonas said. "He says cats don't live to be a hundred. It's biologically impossible. And the white cat we encountered was three years old at the most. She was very young. Feral cats live less than five years in the wild."

Jonas paused. "She?" he asked Neil. "That huge cat was a girl-cat?"

"Yes," CatBob grumbled.

"Then how can Neil explain the fact that both my grandmother *and* great-grandmother had seen the White Phantom in Olentangy Park?" Tallula asked. "That's how I knew the Phantom existed. My grandmother told me about it when I was a kid and her mother did the same. They both said there was magic in the park and that it was guarded by the White Phantom."

"So you expect us to believe that the white cat is a hundred years old?" Jonas smirked.

"Just like you expect me to believe a boy in a chicken costume can talk to cats?" Tallula shot back.

16
CASTLE DUSENBURY

Jonas and his partners looked at one another; their new friend had a point. If Jonas's costume could allow him to talk to cats, maybe it was possible that the Phantom really *was* a hundred years old.

While the detectives considered the possibility that her claim might be true, Tallula retrieved a tome from the bookcase. She sat with the volume laid across her lap and began leafing through it. "Olentangy Park was the largest amusement park in America at one time," she announced.

Jonas and his partners gathered to examine the open photo album.

"These were taken during the time the park was owned by the Dusenbury brothers," she said as she pointed to the photos. "They were the ones that made the park into a major attraction. One of their descendants still lives in Clintonville."

"Yeah, Orville," Jonas said. "He was just telling me about the park's history yesterday."

"So you really do know Orville Dusenbury!" Tallula gasped. "How did you manage to meet *him*? The guy's a total recluse."

"We met him last fall when we were investigating the missing cats," Jonas said. "I'll bet Orville would love to see these photos. Do you wanna meet him?"

"Absolutely!" Tallula squealed.

Jonas took out his phone and began typing a message.

A short time later, the detectives escorted Tallula to Orville's front door. Orville saw the hooded figure looming behind the trio and smirked. "What's this, huh? Did you capture the Ghost of Christmas Future?" he asked.

"Orville, this is Tallula," Jonas announced as he stood between them. "She'll tell you to call her Taco or whatever, but her name is Tallula Kabash Something. She's cool."

Tallula pulled her hood back. "Kobayashi, actually. Tallula Kobayashi." She giggled as she extended her hand to Orville. "But Jonas is totally right. My friends call me Lu-Ko and my sister calls me Ta-Ko, which I don't like, but that's... you know, whatever."

"Tallula," Orville repeated dreamily, "that's a *beautiful* name."

Jonas giggled. Neil was rubbing against Orville's leg, but Orville was too busy looking at Tallula to notice. He just stood there with a goofy grin on his face, as though he had just awakened from a pleasant dream.

Jonas called his cat-friends inside and the trio set off down the hall. Jonas called back to Orville. "Hey, did you smash that Heavy Metal Special already, or is there some left? I'm starving."

Orville snapped out of his trance. "Oh, yeah. I mean, no— I mean, there's some left." He laughed and turned to Tallulah. "Uh, sorry. Come in—please. Welcome to Castle Dusenbury!"

Orville led his guest back to the kitchen where he busied himself unpacking the leftovers from Gatto's in between frantic bouts of cleaning. "So, where have you and the boys been?" he asked Jonas.

"Meeting new neighbors," Jonas answered. "Tallula was showing us a photo album that has pictures of the Dusenbury brothers and we thought you might want to see them."

"Is that right?" Orville said. "Sure, I'd love to see them." He watched Tallula as she craned her head this way and that, looking all around the house.

"Sorry about the house," he called with a cringe, "it's got a mind of its own."

"Oh, please, don't apologize," she said. "This place is living history."

"That's a flattering way to put it," he chuckled, "most people just call it a dump. I had some unexpected visitors last night who party way too hard for me. They kind of trashed the place." He handed Jonas a plate and led everyone upstairs.

When they reached the second floor, Jonas noticed CatBob had once again taken up his post at the end of the hall. He asked the peachy feline if he would join everyone else in the study, but his partner had once again returned to his quiet state. As Orville ushered Tallula into the study, Jonas whispered to CatBob. "You can stay out here, but don't even think of peeing anywhere." Jonas was relieved to see Orville's mood had finally improved and the last thing he needed was another Pee-Pee Cat episode to ruin it.

Orville, Tallula, Jonas, and Neil moved to a clearing that Orville had spent the day carving out of the mess. "Oh, my! This is beautiful!" Tallula exclaimed.

Orville threw Jonas a sidelong glance. "It will be one day," he said. "It'll be my study. But for now, it's my big fat mess."

"Messes are temporary," Tallula said. "It just needs a little organization."

While Orville lit a small fire, Jonas and Tallula moved chairs together and helped Neil up onto Jonas's chair back.

Once the fire was burning and everyone had settled in, Tallula produced the album and flipped to the pages that featured photos of Olentangy Park. She explained that she was a collector of local history and belonged to the Clintonville Historical Society. The Society was a club of history enthusiasts who collected and cataloged relics of historical significance wherever they could find them. She had personally acquired these photos at a warehouse sale. She suspected they had belonged to someone who had either lived or worked on the park grounds.

Orville pointed to the first couple of pictures and confirmed they had definitely been taken during the period the Dusenburys had owned the park. Then he excitedly pointed to a photo of two men standing on either side of a woman.

"That's the Dusenbury brothers!" he exclaimed. "That's John W. Dusenbury, my great-great-grandfather, and that's his brother, Will.

"Who's the smokin' hot mama between them?" Tallula asked. "She's so exotic looking. Her eyes are crazy."

Orville furrowed his brow and frowned. "I don't know. She looks like she might have been a performer, maybe?"

The woman in the photo stood with an arm draped around each of the brothers. She wore an old-fashioned dress and vest, cinched by a large buckled belt. Her dark hair fell in wild tendrils from a jeweled headpiece. But her costume became an afterthought when the viewer saw her eyes. Even in the faded print, they looked almost real. Jonas expected them to blink.

Orville wiped pizza grease from his fingers and carefully plucked the photo from the metal placeholders. He turned it over and discovered another photo was stuck to the back. He gently peeled them apart and the hidden photo slipped from his fingers and went sailing to the floor. Everyone bent down at the same time to retrieve it, but stopped when they saw the image.

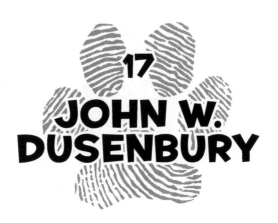

17
JOHN W. DUSENBURY

"Holy—" Orville muttered.

Jonas pinched the photo between his thumb and forefinger and held it out. The image showed a young girl, wearing Jonas's chicken costume, standing next to a pedestal. And on that pedestal was perched a huge, white cat.

Jonas turned the picture over and read the faded writing that had been scrawled on the back. He muttered the name aloud.

"Oláh Gertrud and her cat, Oscar."

Neil gasped.

Orville leaned back in his chair and began wringing his hands again. He gazed at the fire, suddenly lost in his own thoughts. When he came to, he noticed Jonas was watching his hands. Orville immediately sat up and cleared his throat. Then, he reached

over, took the photo of the Dusenbury brothers and turned it over. He read the writing aloud.

"Oláh Dorottya, nineteen twenty-one."

Orville shook his head. "My father never mentioned anyone by that name." Suddenly, he leaped from his chair. "Doc Winslow didn't mention her to me," he exclaimed, "but maybe John W. Dusenbury did!" He hurried to the ladder and flipped on the work lights. "I'm almost certain that John W. Dusenbury's personal journals are *somewhere* in this room. If he knew her, he might have written about her in his journal."

Tallula and Orville immediately set to work sifting through the mountains of volumes stacked by the bookcase. Jonas grabbed Neil and gave him a boost up the ladder, where he hopped on top of the bookcase. A few moments later, Neil cried down to Jonas that he'd found something. A few swipes of his paw sent a dusty tome tumbling into Orville's waiting hands.

Orville wiped the cover and laughed. "Another mystery solved by the Crime Cats!" he exclaimed.

Jonas retrieved Neil and told him to go into the hall and get CatBob, but his cyclopean partner soon returned alone. Jonas looked at him inquisitively, but Neil just shook his head. Jonas hoisted Neil up onto his lap and prepared to translate as Orville settled in to explore the journal.

"My great-great grandfather, John W. Dusenbury, was notoriously sentimental," Orville explained. "He kept detailed journals throughout his life. This one appears to have been started around the time the Dusenburys purchased the beer garden in 1899—see?" Orville pointed to a photo that had been pasted to the first page. It showed the Dusenbury brothers standing proudly before the picnic area by the river on the site that would become Olentangy Park. He flipped through the journal, mumbling as he went, until finally he came to rest on a page that had bare spots where two photographs had been removed. "Here it is!" he announced. He cleared his throat, and then began reading the text aloud.

It is by no minor miracle that I have managed to endure this dark winter without my dear Ellenore. I seem to do nothing but contemplate what misdeed I have committed to cause her heart to change so. She ended our engagement so abruptly that I find it impossible to blame any but myself. But at long last, it seems the bitter frost of sorrow has finally thawed thanks to the mercy of spring's sunshine. Today those dark clouds that have dogged me through these winter months parted and I found myself gazing upon blue skies once again. And as I basked in that glorious glow I thought that perhaps Love had finally taken me in her favor once again.

Will took me to see our newest summer act, a pair that has traveled all the way from Eastern Europe. The first, Oláh Gertrud, is a young lady of only seven, but she exhibits a truly astounding talent. Her cat, Oscar, is the largest feline I've ever seen outside of a zoo enclosure, and he obeys her command as if he comprehends her every word. The cat does flips, jumps through hoops, and performs on a miniature high wire. It's absolutely charming!

After Gertrud's show, Will introduced me to her beautiful mother Oláh Dorottya. (Oláh is a surname, I was informed. In Hungary, last names are put first.)

I found myself at once smitten with her. She possesses the most bewitching eyes I have ever had the divine pleasure of gazing into. Her charms overwhelmed me so that I suffered some embarrassment when I was unable to speak in her presence. I felt like a foolish schoolboy. But she was a lady and very forgiving of my flustered state. Most of our meeting was spent smiling at one another without a word exchanged. I was hopelessly under her spell. However, no sooner had we said our goodbyes than I experienced pangs of guilt for allowing myself to become attracted to another woman. I thought of Ellenore and the undying love I had pledged to her. I considered that perhaps my pledge had been empty and that she was right to leave. How else could another woo me so easily? But I found my conflict short-lived. As soon as Will and I were alone he confided in me that Dorottya had stolen his heart and that he was hope-lessly in love with her.

I said nothing and left abruptly, fearing I might betray my feelings to him. I have spent the remainder of the day in the house, unsure of what to do. Yet all I can think about is Dorottya.

"Aww, poor guy," Tallula said. "It's easy to see why he was in love with her. She was one hot mamma."

Jonas shook his head and grimaced.

Orville plucked out a park program that had been wedged between two pages. It featured an advertisement for "Gertrud and the Amazing Oscar." He passed it around while he continued scanning for more mentions of Oláh Dorottya. After a few moments, he straightened up and continued reading aloud.

My brother's happiness is too precious to compromise. I must master my jealousy and accept that Oláh Dorottya's heart will never be mine. Such is the burden of the bigger man.

"Man, this is rough," Orville sighed, scratching his head. "I had no idea that there had been such a drama between John and Will." He flipped through while everyone else eyed the passing pages. Then he spread the pages flat and announced, "And the drama continued."

Heaven help me! I can stifle my passions no longer. I have tried to ignore her, but I've found her beauty an irresistible force to which I am helplessly drawn. I have even tried to give her cause to look at me less favorably, but she sees through my ruse of ill manners and indignance. I have silently endured the burden of this unending charade for long enough. My heart aches so that I fear it may burst in my chest.

"So then..." Orville mumbled.

I confessed to Will my feelings for Dorottya and told him that I intend to withdraw from our partnership. Will sat patiently through my tearful confession, which ended with my offer to sell my half of the park to him so that I could leave Columbus and not spend the rest of my life resenting him for the happiness he so deserves. When I had finished, he took up the contract I had presented and tore it in two. I was shocked into silence. He then helped me out of my chair and embraced me. He told me that it was not I who must end our partnership, but instead, it was he who would end his partnership with Dorottya. I protested, but Will would have none of it. He said there was no choice in the matter. He would allow nothing to come between us—not even his love for Dorottya.

I arrived home humbled and exhausted by the episode. Later this evening, Dorottya arrived unannounced. She was in tears. She explained that Will had broken off their engagement but didn't say why. This was an awkward position for me, as I dared not disclose the reason to her while attempting to offer what comfort I could.

Then she kissed me.

I recoiled from her touch and her expression suddenly changed. It was then that I knew the true reason for her visit. I had betrayed myself. She became hysterical. She said she knew it was me who drove Will from her arms. It was my jealousy. I remained silent: I could deny nothing—it was all true! She stormed out, wailing unintelligible curses that turned the blood in my veins cold. The guttural noises that croaked from her throat resembled those heard from a wild beast, not a beautiful woman.

Orville looked up from the journal and over to Neil. The feline was purring so loud that Jonas could feel the vibration in his gut.

"Ssshh!" Jonas whispered as he shook the gray cat lightly.

"What?!" Neil meowed.

"You're rumbling up a storm, buddy," Jonas laughed. "Orville can barely read over your purring."

"Sorry," Neil huffed, "I guess I got caught up in the story." He looked over at Orville, who was flipping through pages again. "So tell us what happened to Dorottya and Gertrud."

"Now, let's see—" Orville stopped when he unfolded a piece of paper that had been stuck between two pages. "Oh! What's this?" It was an old newspaper clipping. The paper was brown and brittle, but Orville managed to unfold it and read through it quickly.

"Whoa!" Orville gasped. "It's an article that says Dorottya was arrested for poisoning the pool. It says a judge found her guilty and sent her to the Lunatic Asylum of Ohio.

"Oh, my!" Neil gasped.

"That poor woman," Tallula said. "The heartbreak must have driven her to madness."

"Yeah, and John wrote that soon after, she died there." Orville lifted the journal to his face, examining the writing. "Oh, man. Gertrud was shipped off to live with relatives. Dorottya's belongings were stored." Orville looked up at Tallula. "That must be where these photos came from. Dorottya must have gotten hold of this journal and taken them."

"Or John tore them out," Tallula offered.

"I bet John felt guilty for what happened," Jonas

put in.

"You're probably right, Drumsticks," Orville mumbled as he flipped along. "It certainly wasn't fair that Dorottya had to pay the price for Will and John both falling in love with her, but love is usually unfair." He frowned and examined a series of photos. "Soon after her death, the Stock Market Crash happened and the Great Depression hit. People just stopped going to the park. My father said the only reason John and Will survived ruin was because they kept lots of cash in their houses. But the park pretty much went under." Orville held up some photos taken of the empty park. The writing on the back of the photo read *Saturday, 2:00 PM*.

"Wow!" Tallula exclaimed. "Summer was their busy season. They should have been packed."

Orville grunted in agreement as he flipped through more pages. "Check this out!" he shouted. He held up the book. There was a photo that showed the Dusenbury brothers much older, shaking hands with two other men in suits. "These two guys are Elmer and Leo Heanlein," Orville said. "They leased the park and ran it from 1929 until John and Will sold most of the land to the L.L. LeVeque Company in 1939. This must have been taken on the day the Heanlein boys took over the park."

Neil leaped down into Orville's lap and began

pawing at the journal while meowing at Jonas.

"Neil says to put the journal in your lap," Jonas translated.

Orville did as he was told. The gray cat plopped down on the page and leaned down to examine the photo of the Dusenburys and Heanleins. Then he looked up at Jonas and a let out a string of meows.

Jonas scooted next to the book to join his partner. "No way!" he gasped. "Take a look at what Neil found."

Orville and Tallula leaned in. There, beside Neil's paw was a light spot in the photo. Neil got up and Orville raised the journal closer to his face.

On the far left edge of the photo, a white figure stood close to the ground. It was unmistakably in the shape of a cat—a white cat—watching from just inside the gates.

18
THE
DUSENBURY
CURSE

"This photo would suggest that Gertrud abandoned her cat, Oscar, when her mother was committed," Neil said.

Jonas leaned over the chair's arm, to examine the photo more closely. There was no mistaking it. A white cat was watching the Dusenburys from beyond the park gates. "Freaky," he whispered.

Orville flipped through a couple more pages and halted. "The cat has returned," he announced. He skimmed over the handwriting and frantically flipped through more pages. "Whoa! Listen to this, you guys. After the Heanleins took over the park's operation, John began seeing Gertrud's white cat, Oscar, which he wrote was impossible because Gertrud had taken Oscar with her to New York after her mother's incarceration."

Neil thumped the chair's armrest with his tail. His eye wandered over to Tallula, who was shifting nervously in her seat.

Orville took a sip of his cola and read straight from the journal.

I cannot stand the sight of the beast any longer. If it is indeed a beast that lives and breathes—which I doubt. I am suspicious the Phantom is a demon agent sent to exact D's revenge.

Yesterday I told my groundskeeper that I had seen a large white cat in the yard and I didn't want it digging up the flower beds—and heaven forbid it get into the house with my allergy to the blasted things. Gordon immediately set out spring-loaded traps. But when we went out to inspect the traps the next morning, they had failed to yield anything aside from a couple of frightened squirrels. While we were releasing the squirrels I spied the cat sitting a mere twenty feet away, just watching us. I intentionally directed Gordon's attention to the flowerbed that lay just behind the animal, but it was obvious he didn't see the feline. I, however, immediately went into a fit of sneezing so severe it drove me back inside the house. Will told me he had a similar episode two days prior when the Phantom appeared on the dinner table in the middle of a meal. Will had to stifle his panic so as to not frighten his wife and daughter. He says he's seen it every day since he moved to

California.

I know my sweet Harriet is suspicious something is the matter, but I dare not upset her. I have never told her of D.

"My father never told me any of this," Orville said as he leafed through the pages. He stopped and read silently for a moment before continuing aloud.

...For two weeks I've kept my post at the window at the end of the hall on the second floor. From here, I see the Phantom emerge from the hedgerow every day at dusk. It watches the house for hours on end, sulking in the shadows at the edge of the yard. On several occasions I have attempted to sneak out of the house and catch the thing, but it watches me too closely to be taken by surprise. As soon as I reach the yard I can find no trace of it.

The only solace I have is that Will swears he is experiencing the same phenomenon in California, thousands of miles away. We both see the Phantom—at times simultaneously while engaged in a telephone conversation. But we are the only ones who see it.

Orville gulped. A knot had formed in his throat. He remembered seeing his father sitting at the very same window for two weeks after he'd told him about the white cat in the park. He read on.

...Ten nights ago I heard a scratching at the front door. At first I attempted to ignore it, but found this caused the racket to grow louder and more persistent. After enduring hours of this constant irritation, I flung the door open in a fit of anger only to find an empty porch. However, as soon as I had returned to bed the scratching resumed and the game played out as before.

"A few entries later..."

I have endured thirteen nights of this relentless scratching noise. And no matter to what ends I endeavor to find the culprit, he continues to elude me. The game has deprived me of rest and any peace of mind, but Harriet and Little James have made no mention of the infernal racket. On the contrary, they appear refreshed and happy each morning. Their health and vigor almost mock me.

Orville turned the page and continued, "Two days later he wrote..."

Scratching sounds have multiplied. Last night I heard it at the back door as well—and sometimes at the front and back door at the same time. Now tonight I hear it at the windowpanes and a faint meowing has been coming from the bathroom. When I investigated the source of the sound I discovered it was coming from the sink!

"Two days after that..."

The meowing in the sink is growing louder! The sound carries so that I can feel the vibration in the plumbing pipes. I fear it's only a matter of time before the Phantom will breach the walls. The locks to Harriet's and James's rooms must be secured at night.

Orville continued reading in a strained voice.

My affairs have been put in order and I am ready when the time comes.

The meowing has grown unbearably loud. It sings from every spigot and drain in the house. I shake with fright every time it peals through the halls. There is no escaping it. No place to find any silence or peace of mind.

Orville looked pale as he turned the page and continued.

The meowing has stopped. The house is quiet for the first time in weeks. Yet I see this respite as no blessing. I fear the stillness is the calm before a terrible storm. The anxiety from the anticipation is almost too much for me to bear.

It's here. I heard the unmistakable creak of footsteps on the floorboards downstairs, yet I know no one is down

there. They have moved from downstairs into the stairwell.
They are slow and deliberate, completely unlike Harriet's
shuffle or Little James's energetic gallop, to which I have
become intimately familiar. These steps are altogether
alien to this house and I fear, to this world.

I must now face the Phantom. I am ready.

I hear the scratching, yet when I peer through the crack
under the door, I discover the perpetrator has no physical
form. Not even a shadow is cast in the light.

May God have mercy on my soul.

"That's the last entry," Orville said. The journal slipped out of his hands and smacked against the
floor. "I'm cursed," he muttered.

Jonas looked down at Neil. "Do you think there's
really a curse?" he said.

"Actually," Neil whispered, "I do. But it's not
quite what Orville thinks it is. In fact, the article
from Orville's Science magazine—that I was trying to
tell you about earlier—pertains to this very thing—"

Neil was interrupted by a loud yowl in the
hallway, followed by hissing.

"Oh, no!" Orville cried. "The Phantom—it's
returned!"

Jonas and Neil ran to the doorway. "No, it's
just CatBob," Jonas called back as he and Neil
disappeared down the hall.

"See," Tallula said as she rubbed Orville's back, "no Phantom. You're not cursed."

"But I saw it!" Orville shouted. His eyes took on a wild look. "Here in the house—last night! What am I going to do?" His voice became strained. "How do I break the curse?"

"You need to calm down," Tallula said. She grabbed a paper bag off the floor and offered it to him. "Here, breathe into this."

Orville stuffed the bag against his face and inhaled. "Mmmm," he hummed.

"Is that better?"

"This is the bag my sub came in last night," Orville huffed.

"Oh! Well, we can find another, if you—"

"No," Orville said, sucking the air from the bag, "it still smells like the sub. It had extra cheese. It was so good." He slumped back in his chair. "I'm just sorry there's none left."

Tallula snorted a laugh. "It's okay, I'm not really hungry."

"No," Orville huffed, "I'm sorry because now *I'm* hungry."

19
CRIME CATS, UNITE!

Jonas and Neil marched down the hall where they found CatBob spraying a yellow stream directly under the busted window.

"Oh, no you don't!" Jonas exclaimed as he grabbed CatBob by the scruff. He hoisted the peachy feline under his arm and ran downstairs with Neil trailing behind. "That's it, Bob, you're outta here!" Jonas burst through the front door and flung his friend into a snowdrift.

CatBob reemerged from the snow with his ears pinned back. "What's wrong with you?" he hissed. "It's cold out here!"

"Good," Jonas huffed. "Maybe the snow will snap you out of your Pee-Pee Cat trance. Orville's worried sick about being cursed and losing Castle Dusenbury. He needs our help, not you taking a wizz all over his house."

CatBob hopped from the hole he'd made in the drift. "I'm trying to protect Orville!" he said, shaking off his snow. "The pee is to let them know Castle Dusenbury is off limits!"

"Who is *them*?" Jonas asked.

"The eyes in the bushes," CatBob said in a low voice. Jonas followed CatBob's gaze to the edge of the yard, where he saw two pairs of eyes glinting among the gnarled branches of the hedgerow.

Jonas ran back inside and began jamming on his chicken feet. "Don't take your eyes off of them!" he called. "Don't let them get away."

"Too late. They're getting away!" CatBob called. "Hurry, Jonas!"

"I'm coming," he shouted as he shoved his arms through his coat sleeves.

"Is something wrong?" Orville called from upstairs. "There isn't more pee-pee, is there?"

"Spies in the yard," Jonas panted. "I think they're headed for the park!" He grabbed his gloves, and stumbled through the doorway.

Paw prints had cut a rut through the yard that led to a small opening at the bottom of the wild hedgerow. Jonas caught sight of Neil slipping through the opening and frowned. Even though he could talk to cats, it didn't change the fact the felines could easily outrun him—especially in the snow. That's when he remembered he'd left his sled at Orville's earlier that morning. Jonas turned to find it still leaning next to the door. He grabbed it and made for the sidewalk.

His partners were already crossing to the opposite side of East North Dusenbury where two other cats were quickly trotting down the sidewalk. One was a small longhaired cat with black and white painted markings. As Jonas approached the curb, the cat stopped to look at him with large golden eyes. The feline's markings formed a black handlebar mustache on its white snout. The other cat was gray and so fat it actually resembled a watermelon with legs, a tail, and a head. Jonas couldn't help but smile as he casually jogged across the street.

"Well," he announced as he rejoined his friends, "judging from the size of the gray one, we're not in for much of a chase."

They watched as the large gray cat struggled to navigate the icy patches of the sidewalk on legs that looked much too small for its rotund body.

"Hurry," Ondine yelled as she paused to glance back at the detectives, "they're right behind us!"

"I'm going as fast as I can," Lucy hissed. "It's not my fault it's so slip—*MEOW*!" the grey cat yowled as her tiny legs slid out from under her. She belly flopped onto the hard-packed snow and slid past her

friend. The helpless feline stretched out her legs in an attempt to stop her descent, but icy ground offered nothing to latch on to. "Ondine—help!" she cried.

"Good thinking," her mustachioed companion shouted. "We'll Belly Whopper to safety!" The little cat leaped onto Lucy's back, propelling her over the crest of the hill. Lucy howled as they disappeared from sight.

Jonas took a running leap and hit the snow with the sled under him. "Climb on, guys!" he shouted.

"No way!" Neil huffed. "That will most certainly get— Hey!"

CatBob threw his weight into Neil, sending the cyclopean feline tumbling into Jonas's lap. Then CatBob hopped aboard just as the sled glided over the crest of the hill and began its descent toward High Street. Neil sank his claws into Jonas's snow pants and howled in terror, while his fellow passengers joined in the chorus with howls of glee.

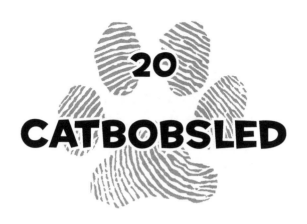

20
CATBOBSLED

The detectives jostled on the sled as they raced down the bumpy footpath. Neil rode in front with CatBob nestled in Jonas's lap as he attempted to steer.

"People!" Neil shouted.

Jonas spotted two adults just ahead. He grabbed the sides and leaned to the left. "Coming through!" he yelled. The sled veered just enough to prevent a collision. He straightened up and then leaned right, bringing the trio back onto the path of trampled snow.

The friends could still see Ondine balancing comically on top of Lucy as the melon-shaped cat glided like a hockey puck over the snow.

"You've been a real jerk to Orville!" Jonas shouted to CatBob.

"I was trying to protect him." his partner called.

"With pee?" Jonas asked. "How did that work out for you?"

"You don't understand!" the peachy feline meowed. "As soon as we got there I smelled those other cats and saw them creeping into the yard. I sprayed under the window to let them know Castle Dusenbury was my territory. I tried to make them leave."

"Car!" Neil shouted.

Jonas saw Ondine and Lucy slide down a curb ramp and disappear behind a black car that had slid to a stop at the intersection ahead.

"Whoa!" Jonas yelled. He clutched the sides of the sled and lifted his legs out. His heels dug into the soft snow on either side of the path, sending a wave of cold dust spraying into the air and onto the sled. The sled turned sideways and finally came to a stop, bumping against the passenger side door of the car. The car's horn honked.

Jonas got up, grabbed the sled, and ushered his friends around the car, reassuring them the car wouldn't *get* them. He waved to the driver and called out apologies. The driver side window came down and a bald fat man's head emerged. He scowled at Jonas.

"*You* again!" the man bellowed. "You're a menace, kid! I could have killed you—you and your little *monsters.*" He pounded on the horn again when he saw Jonas was smiling. "Keep it up, kid. It'll be you, next time!"

Jonas laid the sled down and the detectives piled back on. Within a few moments, they were again speeding down the hill, but Jonas could see that Ondine and Lucy had already reached the bottom.

"Why didn't you ask for help?" Jonas shouted to CatBob.

"I was trying not to upset Neil or Orville," his partner answered. "We were supposed to cheer Orville up since he'd been so depressed. And the dogs that live next door to Neil had been driving *him* crazy."

"Dogs!" Neil shrieked.

"Yeah, I know!" CatBob said. "That's what I was saying—"

"No—DOGS!" the cyclopean cat yowled.

As the sled approached the bottom of the hill, the trio saw that a woman and three large dogs were blocking the sidewalk. The dogs were barking in the direction of High Street, where Lucy and Ondine had darted into the street. The hounds stood on their hind legs, straining against their leashes.

"Look out!" Jonas yelled to the woman as he attempted to dig his heels into the snow again. This time, however, the hardened path was wider and the surface gave nothing for Jonas's feet to dig into. Jonas's heels just slid across the hard surface.

As the woman leaped out of the sled's path, she let go of the leashes. The ends dropped into Jonas's face. He grabbed hold of them just as the dogs made a break for the street, dragging the sled and the detectives along with them.

"Don't let them *get* me!" Neil cried as he climbed up onto Jonas's chest.

Ondine and Lucy had reached the opposite side of High Street and were scampering down the sidewalk. But the pair was now closely pursued by a boy and two cats, riding on a plastic sled that was being towed by three barking dogs. Passing cars slowed as drivers reacted the spectacle with laughs and horn honks. A few people even rolled down their windows to take pictures with their phones. Several long honks in a row caught Jonas's attention. He turned to find Orville sitting in the passenger seat of Tallula's station wagon. He was holding his phone in one hand and giving the thumbs-up with the other.

"This looks so rad!" he shouted. "Keep going. We'll be right behind you, okay?"

"Okay!" Jonas shouted back. He then noticed a scowling face peering out from a backseat window. It was the woman who had been walking the three dogs. "Sorry!" he shouted to her, but the woman just shook her head. Jonas shrugged and turned his attention back to the chase.

"What were you saying about dogs?" Jonas shouted to CatBob over the barking.

"The dogs that live next door to Neil have been driving him crazy," CatBob answered. "I didn't want to stress him out by telling him about the cats. I thought I could keep things under control myself while Orville and Neil relaxed."

The chase slowed as the motley parade turned down West Thurber and careened through the parking lot of the Olentangy Village apartment complex.

"I sneaked out of the house," CatBob meowed, "the evening you found me in the alley. I was trying to stop the Phantom from doing whatever it was she was up to before Neil or Orville found out, but she was expecting me."

"What do you think, Neil?" Jonas asked the gray feline clinging to his coat.

"It may have started out that way," Neil said, "but I think the fight that night hurt your ego more than your hide."

"I agree," Jonas added. "You've been pouting."

"No way," CatBob shot back.

"You gave us the silent treatment and tried to handle the Phantom yourself because, well..." Neil paused. "...because you got beat up by a girl."

"Whatever," the peachy feline muttered.

"Whatever nothing," Jonas returned. "You kept telling me you could handle this, but you couldn't. You didn't trust your friends and you upset Orville."

The sled glided out of the parking lot and through the trees. The friends could see the park just ahead, where Ondine and Lucy were squeezing through the rusty gates.

"We're friends, CatBob," Jonas said. "You started out as a good friend trying to take care of things for Neil and Orville, but—"

Neil cut in. "But you wandered off into a dangerous situation that almost got you killed," he huffed. "Then, instead of letting your friends help you, you pouted because you couldn't take it that a girl beat you in a fight. That's silly—and selfish more than anything."

"How was that selfish?" CatBob asked. "I was protecting you."

"No, you were protecting your ego," Neil spat. "If you were thinking of your friends, you wouldn't have tried to be a tough guy. Instead, you put yourself in a dangerous situation that could have cost you your life."

"Yeah," Jonas said. "Think about how Neil or I would feel if something happened to you."

CatBob looked up at Jonas and meowed. "Well,

maybe I should have told you sooner. I thought I could handle the Phantom myself. I guess I just don't think about you guys worrying about me," he said. "I guess next time I'll ask for help."

Jonas frowned. "Well, I'm sorry I doubted you. I should have known better than to just assume you were being a jerk," he said. "Because I know you're a good guy." He reached down and stroked his partner's head. "Sorry, Buddy."

"I'm sorry, too," CatBob said.

Neil cleared his throat. "All right, Crime Cats! Look sharp."

The sled came to a stop at the gates where the dogs jumped against the fence, barking at Ondine and Lucy who stood on the opposite side. Jonas led the dogs away from the gates and tied the leashes to the fence.

The three friends then slipped through the gates, where Ondine met them at once. The small mustachioed cat crouched in the snow, whining and growling. "Stay back!" she cried.

The trio stopped in its tracks. Jonas slowly raised his hands to signal his peaceful intentions. The sound of coughing drew the detectives' attention to a cat lying in the snow just behind Ondine.

"Someone, help!" Lucy rasped in between coughing fits. "Help me!"

21

LUCY

"You've gotta let us help your friend," Jonas said.

"How— How can you—" Ondine stammered haltingly. Understanding a human's words for the first time had overwhelmed her. Then she paused and shook her head. "No!" she growled. "Stay away! I won't let you hurt Lucy!"

"I promise we won't hurt her," Jonas said. "We just want to help—honest."

The mustachioed cat paused and looked back at her friend, lying prone in the snow. She whined. "Sorry, Luce, I don't know what else to do." She reluctantly stepped aside and motioned for the detectives to approach.

Jonas crouched down and could immediately hear wheezing as Lucy inhaled.

"What do you think, guys?" he asked his partners

who were conducting their own examination.

"She seems to be suffering from physical exhaustion," Neil said. "Running for any distance can be very hard on a cat's body—trust me on that."

"We need to get her warm," CatBob put in.

Jonas nodded. He took off his coat and laid it in the snow, then gently placed Lucy inside and wrapped her up. He cradled the bundle in his arms and stood up.

"You *promise* you won't hurt Lucy?" Ondine asked.

"I promise. You can come along to make sure."

Jonas led the cats back through the empty lot toward the apartments. There, they passed the woman who had been walking the three dogs. She marched by Jonas without saying a word. Jonas shouted his thanks and apologies for borrowing the dogs, but the woman only grumbled as she continued to the fence, where the hounds barked their greetings.

A few minutes later, Jonas and his companions reached the parking lot where they found Tallula and Orville waiting in the running station wagon.

Orville rolled down his window. "That lady was pretty miffed about you swiping her dogs," he called out. "She didn't hurt anyone, did she?

"Nuh-uh," Jonas huffed. "We have an emergency, guys. This is Lucy." He gingerly handed his bundle to Orville. "Neil thinks she's just exhausted from running. You guys have to keep her warm and give her water while we're gone."

Orville took the bundle in his arms and gently removed the coat. "She's so cute," he said as he inspected the melon-shaped feline.

Ondine leaped onto the hood of the car and peered through the windshield at Orville and Tallula.

"Who's *this*?" Tallula asked.

"That's Lucy's friend, Ondine," Jonas said. "She wants to make sure you guys aren't going to hurt Lucy."

Tallula rolled down her window and offered her fingers to the mustachioed cat to sniff. "We'd *never* hurt Lucy. We're friends," she cooed.

After Ondine sniffed Tallula's hand, she walked to the other side and sniffed Orville's as well. After her inspection, she jumped down from the hood.

"Okay, guys," Jonas said as he tugged his coat back on, "just look after Lucy till we get back. Keep her safe and let her rest, okay?"

"Be careful, Drumsticks!" Orville called. He and Tallula waved as they watched the heroes disappear beyond the trees once again.

22
THE BURDEN

The woman and her dogs were gone by the time the friends reached the rusty gates. The park loomed before them, gray and silent, like a frozen graveyard.

"You're not at all like Dasza told us you were," Ondine said.

"Dasza?" Jonas asked.

"Yeah, Dasza. She's the white cat you call the Phantom," Ondine explained. "I don't think you would be friends with Orville Dusenbury if he really was evil."

"We must all understand that Dasza can't help but think those things," Neil said.

Jonas and the cats looked at the cyclopean feline inquisitively. "What do you mean, she can't help it?" Jonas asked.

Neil straightened up. "It's what I've been trying

to tell you, Jonas. Dasza can't help her hatred for Orville—or any Dusenbury—because her hate is programmed into her by her Burden."

"Her *Burden*?" Jonas echoed.

"Yes. It's in the science magazine article!" Neil shook his head. "According to Orville's magazine, researchers have found that if a cat—or even a human—develops a fear of something or someone due to a traumatic experience, that fear can be passed on to their offspring." Neil looked at Ondine. "Felines call this a Burden. It's an intense fear or dislike for something that usually prevents the cat from being harmed by predators in the area in which it was born. But in some instances, it prevents the cat from living a normal, happy life. I suspect that the original Phantom that John W. Dusenbury first saw in the park was not Oscar, Oláh Gertrud's famous cat, but was rather one of Oscar's kittens. One that looked just like him and had inherited Oscar's intense hatred for John and Will Dusenbury."

"So it was Oscar's kitten in the photo behind the gates!" Jonas exclaimed. "But what about John Dusenbury's journal? Both he and his brother, Will, saw the Phantom at the same time—even after Will moved to California and John still lived in Ohio. How was that possible?"

Neil shrugged. "Auto-suggestion, most likely."

Jonas looked at his partner with knitted brows. "What's that?"

"Let's say your mother tells you she saw a rat in your room," Neil began. "Then later, when you're lying in bed, you hear a noise coming from your desk. What would you do?"

"Look for the rat?" Jonas said.

"Naturally. And if you didn't actually *see* the rat—maybe you just saw a shadow moving—you would still assume it was the rat, would you not?" Neil looked up at Jonas. "You assume it's the rat because the rat has been *suggested* to you. That's auto-suggestion."

"I *think* I get it," Jonas nodded.

"Me too, but this rat story is making me hungry," said CatBob, licking his furry chops. "Hurry up and get to the delicious part."

Neil rolled his eye at his peachy partner. "Suggestions are made more powerful when they come from someone you respect and love—someone *you* believe would never lie to you," Neil said coolly. "Your love for that person will make you want to accept what they say as truth. If they insist the rat is real, eventually, you'll convince yourself the rat really exists. And you might actually *see* it—even though it doesn't exist."

"So, in this case, the rat is the lie that the Dusenburys are evil, right?" Jonas said.

"There are a couple of rats in this particular case," Neil answered.

"Aww, come on!" CatBob whined. "This story had better get delicious soon."

"Oh, hush, Bob!" Neil snapped. "The first rat was created when Oláh Dorottya placed a curse on John W. Dusenbury for ending her engagement to his brother, Will. Traditional curse stories usually follow a formula where the victim of the curse is haunted by something symbolic. In this case, the victim, John W. Dusenbury, was haunted by a white ghost cat—a symbol of Gertrud and Dorottya. In reality, there was no curse and the cat he saw was actually one of Oscar's kittens. But when John saw it on the park grounds, he thought it was Oscar's *ghost* haunting him." Neil looked up proudly, obviously enjoying being the center of attention. "Oscar's kitten was likely born with a Burden that caused him to hate the Dusenburys. The young cat likely followed John to Castle Dusenbury and meant him great harm, but it wasn't a ghost. But that didn't stop John W. Dusenbury from convincing himself that he was seeing a white ghost cat everywhere."

"Whoa!" Jonas whispered.

Neil nodded. "Then, John told his brother, Will, that he was seeing a ghost cat. Which in turn suggested to Will that they were under a real curse, and another rat was created. Will Dusenbury sub-consciously convinced himself of everything John had said because he trusted his brother more than anyone else."

"So all of that stuff about the scratching at the door and meowing in the sink..." Jonas said.

"His imagination," Neil answered. "Even his allergic reactions were likely imagined."

"Least delicious story I've ever heard," CatBob said. "Not delicious at all!"

Neil shook his head and continued addressing Jonas and Ondine. "Then there's Oscar's Burden. Oscar obviously blamed the Dusenburys for his family breaking apart. And that belief was reinforced every time one of Oscar's descendants had a kitten that inherited Oscar's Burden. About nineteen generations by my estimation."

"Wow, you sound like Dasza," Ondine said. "She's really smart like you."

Neil flashed a worried glance at Jonas.

"Except she's so angry now," the mustachioed cat sighed. "She's obsessed with taking her revenge on Orville Dusenbury. She said Orville needs to know what it's like to be scared of losing his home."

"Is that why Dasza took Orville's land deed," CatBob asked, "to teach him a lesson?"

Ondine nodded. "She says feral cat colonies have

lived in this ravine for a century. The land belongs to us, not the Dusenburys. It's our birthright." The little mustachioed cat shivered. "But the rest of us don't care about revenge. We just want a home with no more big noisy machines trying to *get* us."

The three detectives looked at one another, silently confirming what none of them wanted to accept: there was no way around it. They would have to face Dasza to get the land deed back.

"We want you to be happy, too," Jonas said to the mustachioed cat, "but we need your help. Do you know where Dasza keeps the land deed?"

23
SNOW CAT

Jonas and his three cat companions cautiously snaked their way through the park until they came upon a dilapidated house. A faint light emanated from the few windows that weren't boarded up. Strange noises crept from beyond the cracked and broken panes.

"That's the Zookeeper's House," Ondine whispered. "That's where we live during the cold season."

"So all of the cats are in there?" CatBob asked.

The mustachioed cat nodded. "And the land deed. Dasza keeps it in her room."

Jonas groaned. "We barely got away when we were out in the open. How are we supposed to enter that house without being—" Jonas suddenly fell silent. He turned to Neil and smiled. "We might not be able to get in, but Lucy could. She lives there."

"Good idea, Jonas," CatBob chirped. "We can roll him in snow and cover up his eye."

"He *is* about the right size," Ondine added. "The snow will make him appear bigger and should mask his scent."

Neil shook his head. "Oh, no! Lucy's *much* bigger than me and I've probably lost some weight from all the running we've been doing lately—"

CatBob leaped onto his friend and pinned him to the ground. "Sorry, Neil," the peachy feline said as he dodged his friend's bites, "but you're the only one of us that has a chance of getting in there."

Neil started to protest, but a glove full of snow stifled his words. He wanted to hiss but stopped himself. He kept his outrage silent because he knew that any loud noise could alert the cats in the house to their presence. He rumbled low growls as Jonas rolled him through the snow. When the indignity was over, Neil was picked up and placed back on his feet.

"Whatever you do, *don't* shake it off," CatBob said. "Tell them you stumbled and rolled into a snowdrift when Orville's henchmen chased you."

Neil began to say something, but Ondine sprinted out of the trees and trotted toward the house. "Hurry up, Lucy, we're late!" she shouted.

"But what if they *get* me?" Neil whispered.

"No one's gonna *get* you. You look like just like

Lucy," Jonas said. "Now go on. We'll be right out here waiting for you."

"You had better be," Neil grumbled as he waddled out into the open.

As soon as Neil strode up next to Ondine, the mustachioed cat whispered, "The deed is upstairs in the first room on the right." She then continued stalking toward the door. "Once you're inside, you're on your own."

The pair followed a rut in the snow that led up a junk pile and through a broken window. When they leaped down from the sill, they were greeted by a group of cats milling around in front of the staircase. The felines looked at Neil and howled with laughter.

"What happened to you, Big Luce?" one of them called.

Ondine glanced at Neil nervously. "She managed to belly flop her way down the sidewalk and into a snow bank," she announced.

The cats laughed until they were silenced by Neil's hiss. The snow encrusted cat shoved through the group and waddled up the stairs.

"All right," the cats cried. "Take it easy, jeez!"

"Catch you later, Luce!" Ondine called out as she sauntered on down the hall.

Neil heaved a sigh of relief. His snow shell had

gotten him inside. But when he looked back down the stairs, he noticed he was leaving a trail of snow chunks behind him. And although the house was cold, it was warmer than outside. His body heat, along with every step he took, was causing his disguise to crumble. He would have to find the deed—and fast—to make it out undetected. He looked nervously around and found the hallway deserted, so he ducked into the first doorway on the right. There was no time to lose.

24
DASZA'S PLAN

Ondine slinked into to what was once a kitchen. The room had been reduced to a sty the colony used for feedings and meetings. It was also the only room that the cats had allowed humans to enter. Pans of kibble were brought daily by a kind woman who lived in one of the nearby apartment buildings, but they presently lay empty and discarded.

A crowd of felines gathered before the counter where Dasza was holding court. The great cat paused in her speech when she saw Ondine enter the room.

"Our scouts return!" she announced. "Report. Has the tyrant Dusenbury learned of our plan?"

"No, Dasza," the mustachioed feline replied. "He hasn't left his house."

"And what of the two feline traitors," Dasza hissed, "and the child?"

A lump formed in Ondine's throat. She paused to swallow hard and said, "Nowhere to be found."

The great white cat pushed her cheeks forward into a triumphant smile. "Excellent!" she chirped. "We have accomplished what nineteen generations of cats have dreamed of: we have won our freedom from the wretched Dusenburys!" Dasza puffed out her chest as the felines below yowled and cheered. "Tonight, we begin the second part of my plan. I'm sure you've all noticed there is no dry food this evening."

Ondine sniffed around at the tins. She had been disappointed that she was going to miss her visit with the woman because of her mission, but it looked as though her friend never showed. Ondine thought that odd, because the woman had never missed a visit in three years.

"No more shall we feed from a human hand!" Dasza announced. "If we are to be independent, we must be so completely. No more kibble. We have turned away the human woman and in her stead I have sent a hunting party into the ravine. They shall return shortly with a bounty from the land." This time, Dasza's statements weren't met with cheers. Instead, the cats all looked at one another and exchanged quick whispers and murmurs.

Sensing the unease of her audience, Dasza

continued. "Brothers and sisters, we will never be independent if we continue to rely on these humans for food. They will only use our dependency against us." Dasza arched her back and loomed over the gathered felines. "I am the nineteenth cat to bear this Burden! It reminds me every day that the Dusenburys are villains. And even after one hundred years they haven't finished scheming against the Glen Echo Destruction. Orville has plotted to take away our home and get us with his great machines. But not this time! This time we have said no! We have struck back! We have taken the power away from him! *We* are in charge now! This land is *ours*!"

The clowder cheered, but Ondine didn't join in. She knew CatBob, Jonas, and Neil weren't bad and neither was Orville Dusenbury. But she felt helpless to stop Dasza or prove to the other cats that her words weren't true. Instead, Ondine shuffled over to the tin pans and sniffed around for discarded morsels. She missed the lady from the apartment complex. She was Ondine's friend and Ondine looked forward to her daily visits. She even came on days when the weather was bad, when none of the cats even ventured out. That's how Ondine knew the lady was a true friend, no matter what Dasza said.

25
ORVILLE'S CONFESSION

Orville's leg bounced like a jackhammer. He gazed out of the window, watching for any movement beyond the trees.

"They'll be okay," Tallula said as she turned knobs and pushed sliders on the dashboard. Hot air blew from the vents with a loud *whoosh*. She turned the deflectors toward the bundle in Orville's arms and grabbed her water bottle. "They know we're here if they need us."

Orville cradled Lucy in his arms and stroked her head. The rotund feline was still wheezing, but her breaths had become steadier, calmer. "I think she has kitty asthma," he said. "I had asthma when I was a kid and cold air can really set it off. My father would always ask me if I had my inhaler with me every time I left the house."

"Mine too," Tallula said, "until I turned twelve. I just stopped having attacks. I ended up running track in high school."

"I did too," Orville chimed in.

"You ran track?"

"No, I turned twelve as well," Orville replied. "I had pretty bad asthma, so running anything was out. In fact, I couldn't do much of anything without wheezing," he mused. "I think I actually had to use my inhaler if I played too many video games."

Tallula snorted a laugh and poured some water into a Thermos lid. "Really? You could have fooled me. Your thumbs are in such amazing shape for your age. I've been trying not to stare." She placed the lid on the back seat. "Honestly, I would have thought you were a former Nintendo Olympian."

A weak smile crossed Orville's lips. "Actually, the only time I didn't have an asthma attack from running happened here," he said. "It was cold out, too. I should have had one, but I just didn't."

"Why do you think that was?" Tallula asked.

"I think I was too scared to have one," Orville said with a rueful smile. "I don't think that's medically possible. But it was a long time ago, anyway. So who knows?" He shook his head.

"No, tell me." Tallula said. "What was it?"

Orville hesitated for a moment. "There's a ravine

back there, behind the park grounds. Have you ever been back there?"

"Sure," Tallula answered. "Who hasn't?"

Orville then told Tallula about the day he was chased by the Thing in the Tunnel. Orville stared into the foggy windshield as he recounted that day, watching it all play out in his mind's eye. "I was so scared," he said, "I could barely think enough to will my legs to move. And the whole time I kept thinking I was going to have an asthma attack at any moment, but I never did."

Lucy began to stir and Orville set her down on his lap. The feline sniffed around and then leaped onto the back seat and began lapping at the water in the Thermos lid.

Orville cleared his throat. "Anyway, I still have nightmares about it. I have ever since." He paused, silently considering something. "I've had much worse things happen in my life since then, but I've never been as scared as I was that day."

"What was in the tunnel?' Tallula asked. "What chased you all the way home?"

"A huge white cat," Orville said. "I thought it was like a feral cat with rabies that just scared me really bad. Until this week I had no idea it was part of a curse on my family."

Tallula began to speak, but Orville cut her off. "I

know it sounds stupid," he waved his hand. "But I've relived that episode a thousand times in my dreams, and every time it feels just like it did that day."

Tallula placed her hand on Orville's. His leg stopped shaking. "I don't think it's stupid," she said. "I think you're brave to come out here and help your friends, considering what you've been through."

"You do?" Orville said, looking at her hand.

Lucy leaped onto the armrest between the seats and meowed up at Orville.

"And I'm not the only one," Tallula said. "You're already Lucy's hero."

26
THE WRATH

Nothing gave Neil Higgins more beastly delight than claiming a piece of fabric as his bed and sleeping on it until it was a disgusting mess of gray fur. But the Zookeeper's House was too much of a mess even for him. The reek of old urine, mildew, and rot stung his nose and eye. His nostrils burned as he rooted through the stained bedclothes, scattered papers, and food scraps that littered Dasza's room. His search came to an end when he pawed open a door to a bedside stand and found the rolled-up document with the words UNITED STATES OF AMERICA printed across it. He snatched it in his teeth and trotted into the hall.

Chunks of snow fell from Neil's fur as he hustled down the stairs. He noticed the right side of his face felt lighter as well. He found the same group of cats at the bottom of the stairs, except this time when they turned to face him, he was met with nasty looks, not laughter.

"What happened to your eye, *Lucy*?" one of them asked.

Neil realized the snow Jonas had packed over his missing eye had fallen off.

"Uh... It was an accident that...." Neil stammered haltingly. As he did, the document fell from his jaws.

"An accident?" one of the cats called. "Must have been a *bad* one. Was it one of the dogs we heard earlier?"

"Actually, it was an.... ice...." Neil stammered out. He was beginning to panic. "...cream cone," he mumbled. "It was so... pointy."

The cats traded bewildered glances, and then one of them began yowling. The others sprang up the stairs. Neil grabbed the document in his teeth and barreled forward, throwing his weight into the advancing felines. The feral cats hissed as they were sent tumbling backward. Neil scrambled up a pile of filthy newspapers and squeezed through a broken windowpane to freedom.

"There he is!" Jonas shouted as he saw Neil emerge from the windowpane. He and CatBob leaped up and rushed to meet their partner, but Neil ran right past them.

"Hey!" Jonas called. "Where are you going?"

That's when Jonas heard a commotion rise from the Zookeeper's House. Terrible caterwauls and hissing grew louder as a line of feral cats spilled from the window and ran straight toward him. He turned to discover CatBob had already taken off after Neil. He stumbled after his friends with the swarm of angry felines nipping at his heels.

The trio weaved their way through the wreckage until Neil stopped and let the document drop from his jaws. He sat in the snow, panting for air. "Can't... keep... running," he gasped.

Strange sounds rose in the night air and surrounded them. Rattling, creaking, and threatening hisses echoed from every scrapheap and every shadowy nook.

"I'm sorry," Neil coughed. "I just can't keep running."

"It's all right, Buddy," Jonas said as he scanned the darkness. "Running won't solve this anyway."

The trio backed up to the entrance of the Scaredy Cat Spook House as darkened figures skulked from the shadows all around them. An angry voice boomed from overhead.

"Surrender the deed and you *might* leave with your skin!"

The trio looked up to see Dasza glaring down at them from atop the giant cat's head. She nimbly leaped down into the snow and turned toward the detectives.

"Hand it over," she screeched, "or face the consequences for your crime, thieves!"

"You stole it from Orville," Jonas shouted. "It belongs to him!"

The feral cats all arched their backs in unison at the mention of their enemy's name. They hissed as the hackles on their spines rose toward the night sky.

"The Dusenburys destroyed my family and now they want to destroy our home," the white feline spat. "This park used to be a place where cats were loved, where magic brought felines and humans together, but the Dusenburys ruined it. We will not let them destroy what we have managed to preserve for the last century!"

"This place might have been forgotten and abandoned, but it didn't destroy the magic," Neil shouted. He turned to Jonas and whispered for him to show them his costume. Jonas unzipped his coat and peeled it off. "That magic still exists!" Neil continued. "And it still brings felines and humans together, it's just not *here* anymore." He looked over at Jonas who now stood in his white feathers.

"The magic lives outside those rusted gates," the cyclopean feline declared, "and it's waiting for you—all of you!"

Dasza gasped as she took in the sight of the costume none of her descendants had seen for almost a century. And even though she had never seen it herself until now, she knew exactly what it was.

"It's working," Neil whispered. "She's beginning to remember."

The feral cats silently watched their leader, waiting for a cue.

"How can this be?" Dasza said. "*You* stole from my family, too?!" The Phantom puffed her chest out and let out a deafening caterwaul.

"I didn't steal it!" Jonas shouted. "It was given to me. The costume must have soaked up Gertrud's power. It's changed me. It made me a true friend to *all* cats."

The Phantom paused. She looked at Jonas and his partners and then she looked upon her feral family. All eyes focused on the great white cat as she considered Jonas's words.

Neil gave Jonas a tail-hug and whispered. "She's trying to reconcile what you're saying and what her Burden tells her. Even though the Burden is a lie, it's all she's ever known. It'll be almost impossible for her to—" he stopped when the white cat spoke.

"A true friend to all cats," the Dasza said, "would never take the deed. A *true* friend would never want our home destroyed!"

With that the great cat bolted through the snow toward Jonas. Before he realized what he was doing, Jonas found himself charging forward to meet her. The pair leaped into the air and collided into a mess of white feathers, fur, teeth, and claws. They crashed into a mound of snow and disappeared from sight. There was a brief sound of screaming and then silence returned.

27
CAT-FRIEND

"What gives?" CatBob asked. "Shouldn't there be scratching and screaming and blood and fur everywhere?"

Neil frowned. "Let's be thankful there isn't." The cyclopean feline took off toward the crater where Jonas and Dasza had landed.

The cats all gathered round and stood shoulder to shoulder in hushed awe. Jonas lay in the snow with Dasza curled up in his feathers, nuzzling his neck. The great cat's purr was so loud that the other felines could feel it vibrating through the snow under their paws. Jonas cooed into the great cat's ear as he gently stroked her head. He looked up at Neil and smiled.

"What happened?" CatBob asked.

"The memories the Burden programmed into

Dasza that made her hate the Dusenburys also enabled her to remember the feathers," Neil said. "Or more importantly, that the feathers were a source of love for Oscar."

"So, what? That's it? The curse is broken?" CatBob asked.

"The curse is broken," Neil said.

"But what about us?" The detectives looked over to find Ondine looking downcast. All of the cats stood with their heads hung, swishing their tails over the snow. "What happens to us—to our home? Where will we go?"

"I'm going to *personally* make sure all of you have a home," Jonas said as he rose to his feet. He gently sat Dasza down and stroked her back.

The white cat looked around at the worried faces and let out a sob. "I'm so sorry," she meowed. "I was only trying to save our home. I was doing what I thought was best."

"We know that," Ondine said as she licked Dasza's head. "You did the best you could and we're lucky to have someone looking out for us, but not everyone's right all the time." Her family gathered around and nuzzled the sobbing feline.

Tallula flipped a switch and the car's headlights revealed Jonas and his partners being followed by a small army of cats. Orville gasped when he caught sight of the large white feline. He opened the door and gently set Lucy down on the ground.

Ondine ran out to meet her friend. "I knew they wouldn't get you," she cried. The two rubbed their faces together and then joined the rest of the clowder behind the detectives.

"So," Orville stammered nervously, "did you get the deed?"

Jonas produced the rolled up paper and waved it. When Orville reached out to take it, Jonas jerked it back.

"Not so fast," Jonas said. "There is a *big* condition to getting this back."

"What kind of *condition*?" Orville asked.

"I have a few friends that need some help finding a new home, "Jonas said. He stepped aside and motioned to Dasza, who hesitated when she saw Orville. Then she padded over to him and gave a timid meow. "This is Dasza," Jonas said. "She and her family need a place to stay for a while. And before you say no, I talked with Neil and we both think you two just got off to a bad start."

Orville looked down at Dasza and then over to the trio. He took a deep breath and extended a trembling hand. Dasza sniffed his fingers.

"See, Orville, Dasza isn't a phantom cat,

Jonas said. "Neil figured out she's a descendent of Oláh Gertrud's amazing cat, Oscar, but she's only about three years old." Jonas then turned to address Dasza. "And Orville's family never wanted to hurt anyone. In fact, both of the Dusenburys were in love with Oláh Dorottya, but jealousy threatened to destroy their relationship, so they chose their family over her."

"That's right," Neil added. "Dorottya was driven to madness by heartbreak. She poisoned the park's pool and was arrested by the police. Afterward, it was a judge that had her locked up, not the Dusenburys."

Orville gritted his teeth as his fingers made contact with Dasza's fur. He felt the vibrations of her purr and smiled. She sniffed his hand and then rubbed her head against his palm.

Jonas smiled at the two. "So, do you think you can make some room at Castle Dusenbury for new friends?"

Orville looked over the motley horde. "I think I can move some stuff around... with some help," he said, smiling at Tallula. "What do you say?"

"I'd love to." Tallula giggled and batted her eyes.

"Ugh—gross!" Jonas said. "All right, let's go home."

28
NEW NEIGHBORS

Orville signed off on the sale of the old park, but he added some stipulations to the contract. Any salvageable structures left over from Olentangy Park were to be donated to the Clintonville Historical Society to preserve and care for, with the exception of the giant cat's head from the Scaredy Cat Spook House. That, Orville took for himself. He said he intended to have it restored and fitted around the back door of Castle Dusenbury to go with the new cat flap he was planning to have installed.

Orville was back to his old self—or would have been, if he hadn't been so in love with Tallula. Their constant exchange of giggles and goofy smiles grossed Jonas out, but he was still happy to have his friend back. Unfortunately, most of Orville's time was spent cleaning, organizing, and supervising the workmen who began renovating Castle Dusenbury, so Jonas didn't get to see him as much. In fact, no one did. After an exhausting day, Orville usually ended up passed out in his recliner in front of a cozy fire with Dasza curled up on his belly and the rest of his feline houseguests basking in the heat.

It was on one of those evenings that Orville again dreamed of being chased by the Thing in the Tunnel. But this time, when he woke up, he found Dasza licking his nose. In that moment, Orville's terror melted. He stroked her face until they both fell back asleep. He never had that dream again.

About a month later, the Shurmanns received an envelope addressed from Castle Dusenbury. It was an invitation to a dinner party. The card stated that it was being held in honor of CatBob, Neil, Jonas, and Mr. and Mrs. Shurmann. The dress code specified that guests were to wear "their favorite Heavy Metal concert T-shirt."

Jonas and his family arrived at the appointed time on a Friday evening with CatBob and Neil in tow. Jonas's parents had worn their favorite Heavy Metal T-shirts as requested and had bought Jonas one for the occasion. Jonas's mom used the opportunity to purchase novelty concert T-shirts for CatBob and Neil, so they wouldn't feel left out. Well, that's what she told Jonas and his dad. The truth was, she always

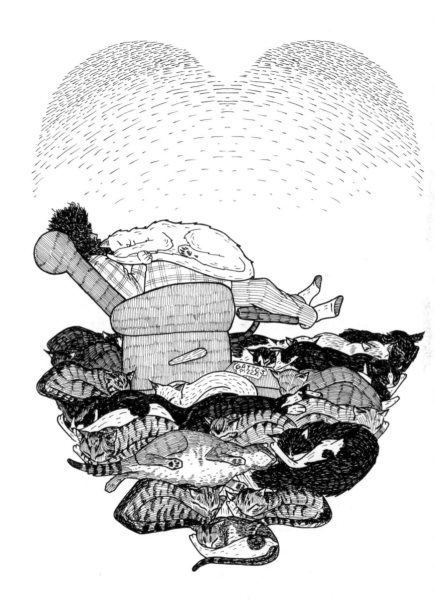

wanted to buy them and finally had an excuse.

Tallula answered the door and Jonas made introductions. Once everyone was out of their coats and cat carriers, Tallula ushered the guests through the house, where they were shown the results of the renovation efforts. Jonas was amazed. Castle Dusenbury was starting to look like a normal house. The cobwebs had been cleared, the old tattered rugs had been thrown out, and there wasn't a cardboard box or junk heap in sight. Shelves had been dusted, floors had been swept and polished, and the usual musty smell had been replaced with the decidedly more pleasant aroma of sawdust.

"And this is just the beginning," Tallula said. "A crew will be here next week to assess the house from foundation to roof. Then the real work will begin."

"The place looks awesome already!" Jonas exclaimed. Even his feline partners were amazed by the change. They busied themselves sniffing the floor and climbing up on everything to get used to the new surroundings.

"This really is something," Mr. Shurmann piped up, "but where is the Lord of the Manor, anyway?"

"He's making our dinner... arrangements," Tallula giggled. She directed the guests' attention to the top of the stairs where Orville stood, clad in a faded black T-shirt with an eagle screen-printed across the front. A silk smoking jacket hung open over his shoulders. He leaned casually against the banister, holding a curved pipe in one hand and his phone in the other.

"Yes, my good man," he said into the phone. "That's right, two Heavy Metal Specials. Capital! I shall see you then." He slid his phone into the pocket of his brocade jacket and bit down on the end of the pipe as he studied his guests. Bubbles spewed out of the pipe and cascaded down to where CatBob and Neil attacked them. "Thank you, ladies and gentlemen, for accepting my invitation," he said. "I trust Miss Kobayashi has shown you around the house. It is the beginning of the Great Restoration that we celebrate tonight. For over 100 years Castle Dusenbury has stood watch over East North Dusenbury Street, but not all of them proudly. Most of Clintonville's residents think of her not as a jewel, but as an eyesore. However, as you can see tonight, she is on her way back to her original glory and that would have never happened without you, my friends."

Orville scooped up Dasza and cradled her in his arms. "Tonight, I wish to express my gratitude to my friends, human *and* feline, alike. For without you, I wouldn't have been able to remain in my home, nor would my world have been filled with so much love."

Twenty more sets of paws padded down the stairs

to meet the guests. CatBob and Neil sniffed noses with the clowder and rubbed cheeks. The Shurmanns crouched down, petting fuzzy heads and cooing greetings. Once everyone had said their hellos, Orville leaned over the railing and cleared his throat loudly.

"Drumsticks," he said to Jonas, "would you be so good as to translate for our feline guests?" Jonas nodded and crouched down to where his cat-friends sat.

"I've brought you all together this evening to express my thanks," Orville announced. "Each of you has had a hand—or paw—in making me one of the luckiest guys on Earth. CatBob and Neil Higgins have been my friends since I moved back to Clintonville and began my evening strolls. Back then, I had no idea how important they would be in my life. I just liked that they always managed to make me feel better by visiting with me, no matter my mood when I set out." Orville then looked over at Jonas's parents. "And that brings me to Mr. and Mrs. Shurmann. Thanks to them, Jonas made friends with CatBob and Neil, and it was through their partnership that Jonas entered my life. Had these three detectives not set out to find the missing cats, none of us would be standing here today, because the bank would have foreclosed on this house and I have no idea where I would have ended up," he said, looking down at the floor thoughtfully. "And it was their friendship, once again, that brought peace to my world—and brought me new friends." Orville smiled as he looked at Tallula and then over to the clowder of cats that patiently sat, watching him and intently listening to Jonas's whispered translation. "Although the newspapers will never write about this latest case—because, as they say, if you didn't see it, you won't believe it—it deserves a celebration. Because of the bravery, dedication, and brains of the Chicken-Boy of Clintonville and the Crime Cats, the Dusenbury Curse has been broken and my family's home has been saved. And they have brought new friends into my life and..." Orville paused and smiled bashfully. "...a new love."

Tallula sighed and wiped the tears that had welled in her eyes.

"So, Drumsticks, CatBob, Neil -- get up here," Orville called, motioning to the trio.

Jonas and his partners scrambled up the stairs and took their places beside Orville. Mr. and Mrs. Shurmann looked on, leaning on one another and smiling proudly. At their feet, the clowder sat quietly, patiently admiring the heroes. Jonas translated for Orville as he continued.

"So, tonight we shall enjoy a banquet in honor of our neighborhood heroes. Beast Feast for our feline friends and Heavy Metal Specials for our human friends." Orville raised his hand and motioned to Tallula, who was stationed at the turntable, ready to drop the needle onto the spinning record. "So I ask you all to join me in the age-old Dusenbury tradition of expressing thanks for friends and family with some sweet, delicious... METAL!" Orville's screech was joined by loud caterwauls. Tallula lowered the needle onto the record and the stereo speakers exploded with thundering drums and wailing guitars.

Orville led his guests in ridiculous dances and air guitar antics. Even the cats joined in. They leaped on furniture, swished their tails, and ran around the house, yowling along with their human friends. The fact that their feline ears couldn't recognize music didn't matter. The clowder's new friends had showed them that anger isn't worth holding on to and that love can heal old wounds. And they could think of no better reason to celebrate than to give thanks for the good fortune they had been afforded.

"PEE-PEE CAT"

If your cat-friend is urinating outside of his/her litter box, you need to pay attention. They are trying to tell you something is wrong. Sometimes the cause of this behavior is physical and sometimes it's mental. Here are some pointers to help you figure out what this stinky message means so you can remedy the problem and get back to enjoying your cat-friend's company.

1. Veterinarian. Take your cat-friend in for a check-up. Be sure to write down exactly where and when your cat-friend is peeing in the house. The more the vet knows, the more easily he/she will be able to identify the cause as a physical or behavioral issue.

2. Sore feet. Sometimes after a cat is declawed, their feet become very sensitive. Many find stepping on clay litter painful, so they pee elsewhere. Litter made of wheat or other softer material may ease this pain. If your family is considering having your cat-friend declawed, I recommend you research first. Declawing is often a painful and even traumatic surgery for cats to endure.

3. Dirty litter. Litter boxes should be cleaned at least once a day. You wouldn't want to use the bathroom if no one in your house flushed the toilet for a week, would you? Help your cat-friend by scooping their litter box once a day. They will appreciate it.

4. Covered litter box. Covered litter boxes don't give your cat-friend more privacy. They only make cats feel confined and hold in stink. Humans experience the same thing when they use a Porta Potty on a hot day. Yuck! An appropriately-sized litter box with no cover is better.

5. Location. Never place the box anywhere near where your cat-friend eats. Damp basements, closets, and anywhere near appliances that can frighten cats are big no-no's as well. If you have more than one cat in your home, consider having a couple of boxes in different places. Some cats don't get along and they may not want to cross the other's path to get to their litter box. The best location is where your cat-friend will feel safe and have some peace and quiet while they do their Secret Butt Stuff.

6. Litter Brand. There are litters made with herb attractants blended in them that draw cats to the litter box. They work quite well and can be a valuable tool for retraining cats who have developed bad habits due to previous physical or behavioral issues.

"ADOPTING A STRAY OR FERAL CAT"

In the story, Jonas, CatBob, and Neil encountered a colony (or destruction) of feral and stray cats. When Dasza agreed to return the land deed, she made Jonas promise to help her family find a home. You may discover similar colonies of cats in your area and want to help them, but before you do there are things you must consider.

1. Stray cats. Stray cats are felines who have been socialized to people at some point in their life. Stray cats are usually adoptable and can easily learn to live indoors with humans.

2. Feral cats. Feral cats are not socialized to humans and will not likely adjust to life indoors. There are exceptions, but it depends on the cat.

3. Feral kittens. Kittens born of a feral mother can easily be socialized to humans and become pets.

4. Tell the difference. Stray cats are cats that have been abandoned by their human family. They tend to be dirty, scared, and when they are approached they will likely greet you like a pet cat: tail up as a sign of greeting. A feral cat will have a clean coat, but it will not greet you like a pet. It will stay low to the ground and wrap its tail around its body. This is a sign it wants to be left alone. You should not attempt to touch a feral cat.

5. No-kill shelters. Use the Internet to find no-kill shelters in your area and take a cat that you suspect is a stray there or to your local veterinarian. Both places can check to see if your cat-friend has been microchipped. This is the best way to find the cat's home. However, if they have no home and you have to leave your new cat-friend at the no-kill shelter, they will have a much better chance of finding a forever home than they will at a normal shelter.

6. Trap-Neuter-Release. Many shelters have Trap-Neuter-Release programs where feral cats are humanely trapped and then neutered/spayed and vaccinated. This is done to keep the cats from getting sick and prevents them from having any more kittens. While at the shelter, experts will decide the degree of the cat's socialization. If the cats are socialized to humans, then the shelter can work to find them a home with a new family. If the cats are too feral, the shelter will return them to their home in the wild.